JACK ON THE TOWER
A Jack of All Trades novel

DH Smith

Earlham Books

Published 2017 by Earlham Books
Book design & cover art by Lia at Free Your Words
(*www.FreeYourWords.com*)
Cover photo: massonforstock at 123RF Stock Photo

ISBN: 978-1-909804-25-8

PART ONE:
TWO HOUSES IN FOREST GATE

Chapter 1

The sand had arrived in a large, open glass-fibre sack, left on the pavement just outside the gate. Beside it were a stack of cement bags and a four litre container of plasticizer. Jack was annoyed at their carelessness at leaving it out. But it was all there; maybe thieves get up late.

So much of it. All to be made up and squeezed into the spaces between the bricks. Pointing was the most boring job on earth. Every brick of the house was embedded in mortar, open to attack by the weather, in this case, for more than a hundred years. No wonder the mortar was flaky, with holes and gaps. But boring or not, he needed the work, and they'd accepted the price. A job was a job. For five or six weeks, depending on the weather.

All he could do was get on with it, and hope something more challenging came up in the work to follow. He looked at his watch. The scaffolding tower was due in half an hour or so. He'd best make himself known to his employer. He brushed down the top of his paint-stained overalls to no observable effect, and flicked back his curly brown hair, receding a little at the brow. And looked up at the clouds. Floating cumulus and stratus. He'd become quite a cloud watcher as a builder, much of it working outside, preferring it to work inside. More room for sawing and planing, no one watching for scratches you might make on the piano. But weather didn't always allow that freedom. Hence his cloud watching, useful too for his astronomy, for which the ideal was clear skies, or the usual compromise – some clear sky. The weather though was pleasant, the tail end of summer which any day could feel the blast of autumn.

Here's hoping.

Jack needed to get this lot undercover. The sand would

be all right but wet cement would set in the sacks. There was a shed in the back garden he'd been told he could use. Best tell the house he was on site. After that, put the cement in the dry. Then wait for the scaffolding tower to come. It was always surprising how much you had to do before you could actually start work. If it wasn't stacking up materials, it was waiting for something vital to arrive.

Jack climbed the half-dozen steps to the front door, and looked up at the portico surrounding the door with its mock classical pillars, an arch over them with floral flourishes in the plaster work, one of the many variations for the Victorian houses on the road.

He'd put in a cheap estimate to get the work. Not that he really wanted it, just needed it. Quite a mood he was in this morning, the overlay of last night. It had hit him watching a talk show on TV; what he wouldn't do for a drink. For several months, he'd been clear of such thoughts, but the untidy flat, the inanity of the celebs on the sofa, and he was struck by a wave of depression. Not assisted by the thought of six weeks of pointing. He'd phoned up Max, his mentor from Alcohol Halt. Max had come over and talked to him for an hour. Bless him.

And really things weren't that bad, not bad at all in fact. As Max had said over and over. He was working, off booze, his health good, more or less solvent, his daughter fine. No love life but that didn't mean never, just no one at the moment.

How would getting drunk help? asked Max. The answer was mundane. It did and it didn't. While you were blotto you had not a care in the world. But when you woke up, you were yourself again, same hassles, same universe, and with a hangover to boot.

Max and he had talked; well, mostly Max talking, Jack nodding. Finally he'd pushed Jack into the shower, and once out he'd felt a lot better, coming into the sitting room to hear Tracy Chapman singing *Fast Car*. A song for the road, with a woman by your side, on the journey to hope. He mattered, Max told him. Things would get better.

Until the morning.

He must busy himself. Quit the self pity. Max was 100% right. He must see what he had, not what he hadn't. Meet people, look them in the eye. You have every right to be living on the planet, Jack. And other fortune cookie slogans.

Jack rang the doorbell, just as the front door opened. Before him was a woman in a navy blue business suit over an open-necked, white shirt. Her face was pink and youngish, with layered, reddish-brown hair, obviously rushing and halted only by his presence.

Jack was stuck for words. Was she a visitor or did she live here? She looked like a banker or a solicitor.

She spoke first. 'Our builder, I presume.'

Jack smiled in relief. He'd placed her. She was the woman of the house. It was good to be expected.

'Yes. Jack Bell. And I'll be around for some time. I thought I'd come and show I was on the job.'

'My husband, Mike, took you on,' she said with a nod.

'That's right. I was here early last week to do the estimate. It's your signature on the contract, Jean Lucas, I got in the post?'

'Yes, it is. I'm Jean. Pleased to meet you, Jack,' she said biting her lip and looking at her watch. 'I really must go. Sorry to be unsociable. Usually I work from home... but I have an appointment this morning. I'll see you around.' She turned and called into the hallway. 'Mike! The builder's here.'

And she was clipping down the steps in her black three-inch heels. Jack waited at the open door to be invited in. On one side of the hallway were two long pine shelves, held up by bricks at the ends. On the bottom shelf and on the floor underneath were a variety of outdoor shoes: boots, trainers. On the top were hats, male and female and unisex. On the other side of the hallway was a child's pushchair.

A head poked out of the first door in the hallway. Youngish, with straggly fair hair, and in need of a shave. Jack recognised him from last week.

'Come in, mate,' called the head.

Jack wiped his feet on the mat and entered. It was important to be polite and exude confidence, especially in first meetings. Politeness came easy enough, confidence though was a trick he was sometimes better at than others. Today he was at the negative end, as if he could see his future stretched out over a tundra of pointing jobs to a gravestone on the horizon. Forget the fictitious future, insisted Max, see the instant, here and now. That's enough. Try meditation. Max swore by it.

Never worked for Jack. Max told him he wasn't doing it properly. At such points he preferred Max washing dishes.

Work. That did the trick. Mostly.

He stood at the doorway of the sitting room.

'Hi, Mike,' he said brightly. 'The sand and cement have arrived. I'm just waiting for the scaffolding.'

'Then how about a coffee?'

Mike was seated on the pale brown leather sofa. He had striking blue eyes and was wearing a dirty green T-shirt under a denim jacket. His jeans were torn at the knees. The room was uncomfortably tidy which was why Jack was at the door, not wanting to invade. The only untidiness was created by a child on the carpet doing a jigsaw with very large pieces. All the books were shelved, the items squarely on the mantelpiece as if spaced out to the inch, the floor and carpet achingly clean, two large abstract paintings on the walls precisely in the middle. One half of the room, almost to the French windows, had a long, dark polished wooden table with six high-backed matching chairs. A huge television set was on with a man and woman walking around a largely empty room.

4

'I should get the cement into the shed,' said Jack with a wave of his arm in the direction of the clouds. 'In case of rain.'

'Have a coffee first,' insisted Mike, rising. 'We'll have it on the patio.' He turned to the child. 'Come on, Lily. We'll go outside.'

Lily got up on her stumpy legs and took his outstretched hand.

'She's not talking,' added Mike. 'A good listener though.'

He led his daughter down the sitting room to the French windows. Jack followed, aware of his boots on the carpet and polished floorboards. Mike opened the windows, put his head out for a moment and pondered.

He turned to Jack. 'Look after Lily for a moment while I get her coat and bring out our coffees.'

Mike turned back into the house while Jack went on to the patio with Lily. Jack sat down on a bench and thought, Mike shouldn't do this. He didn't know Jack, and really shouldn't leave his daughter with a stranger. The child was on a little three-wheeler bike and was driving around the patio between the furniture and the pots. There was a rattan table with four matching chairs. Smart, but Jack wondered how it stood up to the weather. He supposed, it being plant based, that it would survive for a few years. Then they'd burn it and buy something new.

The garden was easy maintenance. Mostly lawn, with two edges planted out with roses, some blooms still, and to the front of the bed, tired geraniums. The shed was down at the bottom. He hoped there'd be room inside for the cement. He wanted to get working but reckoned it did no harm getting to know the homeowner. It was with him that he'd have to talk through any problems. Or maybe the wife. The little he'd seen of her, she'd looked tougher in her business suit. Couples can be difficult. You have to know which one makes the decisions.

Mike came out with the coffees on a small tray plus a child's cup of juice. Also on the tray was tobacco, a lighter, cigarette papers and a lump, of what Jack presumed was cannabis, in silver foil. Over his shoulder was a child's coat. Mike put the tray on the table and beckoned Jack over.

Jack joined him at the table.

'Nice out here,' he said.

'Gets me out of the house,' said Mike with a smile. He was putting the coat on Lily who was reluctant to get off the bike. He coaxed her in that half-baby language, so embarrassing in front of strangers. With one arm in, she resisted and Mike snapped at her. Not quite so laid back, thought Jack. Mike pulled at Lily in annoyance and pushed her into the coat. Jack was tempted to say something but knew it wouldn't be welcomed. He drank his coffee.

His daughter's coat on, Mike came back to the table. He was good looking, if untidily so. Jack supposed they were the same age. His face was taut with impatience after his little battle, but broke into a smile as he sat down.

'I'm the house husband. Jean is the breadwinner,' he said. He pulled towards himself the items for rolling a joint, fixing three Rizla papers together as he spoke. 'I'm a musician. I did eight years with the show *Liverpool Lullaby*.'

'Up the West End,' said Jack, recalling the show. ''60s Liverpool scene with flower people, something like.'

'Yeh. The Beatles crossed with *Hair*, with a love story between a Vietnam deserter and a hippy earth mother. Pure drivel. Nice music for the first few months. Then a drag. Oh, what a drag. You cannot believe how boring it had become by years 6, 7 and 8.' He stopped and smiled as he sprinkled tobacco on to the cigarette papers. 'But it paid well. Got this house between us. I played keyboards and guitar, sang a bit. And now I'm resting, between looking after Lily.'

'I've a daughter,' said Jack, thinking he should contribute. 'Thirteen now. Lives with her mum, but I see her pretty often.' He watched Mike crumbling the weed into the spliff, and wondered if he always began the day this way. Not good, like morning drinking, a way to do nothing.

'I haven't worked for 18 months,' said Mike. 'Unless you call this work. I am a kept man. She makes the money. I spend it.' He had put cardboard in the end of the joint and was licking the paper edges. Jack watched the artisan who was plainly pleased at his handiwork.

'What does your wife do?'

Mike smiled, the joint in his fingers ready to go. 'She's an entrepreneurial zoomer.'

'Sorry...' said Jack.

'One of these new online wizards. You must have come across them. She writes fantasy and blogs and runs Skype courses. I can't keep up with her. Two years ago she was nothing and then bingo – she hit the method. Now she is so busy, her books on Amazon and Kobo, sending out fan newsletters, making up videos. This morning she's off to see an agent. In another year, she'll be taking over Europe. In two, the northern hemisphere.'

Mike lit the joint with the lighter and sucked in deeply. He closed his eyes as the smoke went down and the drug began to bite. He held it in for some time, then blew out the remnant of smoke and took another long drag, and then a third. Contentment radiated from his face to his limbs as he held out the joint.

'No thanks, I've scaffolding coming. Did you sort out next door about the fencing?'

Mike gave him a lazy smile. 'I thought I'd leave that to you.'

Thanks for nothing, thought Jack. OK. He'd got the measure of the househusband, stoned before nine in the morning, far too preoccupied to talk to a neighbour. Nice house, busy wife. He wondered how that worked. Jack's phone rang. A call he was expecting.

'Jack Bell,' he said.

'Got your tower outside.'

'I'll be right out.' He switched off the phone and jumped up. 'Scaffolding has come. Better get out there.'

'Take the side door,' said Mike pointing the way with a lazy hand.

'Right. Thanks for the coffee.'

Jack strode off the patio down the path between the two houses. There was the fence he'd have to negotiate about. He needed this section down to have room to put the scaffolding tower up. Unfortunately, it belonged to the neighbour.

He opened the back door, and put it on the latch as he would need to be in and out with the cement and then the tower. Once he'd sorted out the fence which should have already been done. Mike had most definitely said 'leave it with me.' Yeh, well.

In the street, at the front of the house, was an open backed lorry with two men in green overalls and yellow hard hats awaiting him.

'Where'd you want it?' said one, obviously in a rush, making Jack realise how much he'd slowed to match Mike's pace.

'Put it in the front yard.'

The yard was paved over, so nothing to damage. The men set to laying out the elements that made up the scaffolding tower. Jack would have helped but could see at once that they knew exactly what they were doing and he would've been a hindrance. In a minute or so they'd offloaded the pile of aluminium poles, metal sides, platforms and the bag of fittings. Jack signed for it, hoping it was all there. Though how could you tell on sight if anything was missing? You'd only find out once you'd got to the end point of the assembly. Better be there. £140 a week it was costing him. They left Jack with a booklet and were gone.

Jack looked at the tidy pile. Quite a jigsaw, but he'd assembled towers a number of times, even been on a course. It wasn't complicated, and quite logical. Though a chore on his own, especially the top sections. Just don't rush it.

Cement bags first. He didn't trust that sky.

Jack got the wheelbarrow out of his van which was parked a little way up the road. He wheeled it to the bag of sand and mound of sacks. He put two 25kg sacks of cement in and headed through the garden door, past the side of the house and the patio where Mike was still smoking. He'd moved to the bench and was reading Lily a story out of a big picture book. He gave Jack a wave.

Jack took the path down the garden, along the fence. Halfway down, over the fence, he spotted a man in the next door garden. He was building something at the end. He glimpsed a concrete mixer. Jack would dump these sacks and have his necessary word with the man.

The shed was, of course, full. Standard for sheds. They begin with the best of intentions, but gradually become a muddle, that grows worse as there is no room for anything, and the next items are pushed in anyhow. Jack spent ten minutes throwing deckchairs, timber, buckets, bicycle wheels further in, to clear some space at the front. He had complete freedom as none of it was his, and so he didn't know, or care, what was wanted when, or if it ever would be. His only responsibility was to his sacks of cement.

Once he'd made space, and laid the first two bags, he crossed to the fence to talk to the man in the next door garden. Jack watched him a little while. The man was shovelling sand into the concrete mixer. Jack could see at once by the neatness of the string lines and boards, to hold the cement in place, that he knew what he was doing.

'Excuse me,' called Jack. 'Can I have a word?'

The man put down the shovel and came over. He had a bulbous nose that looked as if it had been broken in a fist fight, thick lips in a swarthy and weathered face, and a full head of dark greying hair. He was medium height, wearing a vest and jeans.

'How can I help you?' he said, in an accent Jack was pretty sure was Polish.

'Nice bit of work you're doing there,' said Jack.

The man shrugged nonchalantly. 'I'm building a shed.'

Jack knew at once it was more than a shed. Too big altogether. An oblong laid out, almost the size of a house. He guessed the man might have less-than-legal plans. Round here in the big gardens, dodgy landlords were letting out sheds to take advantage of the housing shortage. He'd best mind his own business if he wanted to get on the man's good side. Hoping he had one. And then he considered – was he talking to the right man? He could be just a builder, like he was.

'Is that your house?' he added, pointing to the dwelling at the front.

'That's mine,' he said. 'And I guess you are Mike and Jean's builder.'

'Yes, I am. Doing the pointing. I'm putting up a scaffolding tower to do the side wall. And the alley is too narrow unless I take your fence down. I'll put it back up again, it just slots out. Well, you know that.'

'Four hundred pounds,' said the man.

'Sorry, I didn't quite catch you.' He had, but hoped he hadn't.

The man smiled and wiped his sandy hands on his jeans. He had a single gold tooth in the centre of his upper teeth. 'I want four hundred pounds for you to put your scaffolding tower on my property.'

Right first time. Jack took a big breath. Could the man be serious? The fencing panels simply slotted out. They'd not be damaged. On the other side was just paving stones, ample support for the tower. He'd clear up, he'd hardly be in the way.

'That's ridiculous,' said Jack. 'You don't have to do anything. There won't be any mess.'

'It's my property,' insisted the man.

Jack sighed and considered his options. He hadn't anticipated this, expecting neighbourly assistance. Naïve of him. The man was stocky, tough, and waiting, watching Jack, sizing him up as much as Jack was him.

Jack said, 'If you're going to be difficult, I can do the pointing from a ladder and stay out of your property.'

The man smiled wryly and nodded. 'It will take you twice as long. And you'd risk your neck.'

Jack all but swore, holding his thoughts in. The man was a total bastard but he was right. There was no way Jack could pay him four hundred. That was a big chunk of the money he hoped to make on the job.

'Be reasonable.'

The man shrugged.

'I could report you,' said Jack desperately, 'for not having planning permission for your shed.' The man winced and Jack knew for certain what was going on. 'And for its intended use.'

The man strode towards Jack. Stepping into the flower bed, he poked Jack in the shoulder with a forefinger. 'You do that and I'll kill you.'

Jack stood his ground, the man's head barely a foot from his own. He could smell garlic sausage on his breath.

'Kill me,' he said, 'and you won't make four hundred. Most likely you'll be inside for twenty years.'

The man took half a step backwards and put out his hand. 'Feliks.'

Jack was unsure what was happening. Some concession? He took the man's hand and they shook.

'Jack.' It was a strong grip; they were surely testing each other.

He released Jack's hand. 'Make me an offer.'

Jack thought for a few seconds, what was too high, what was too low? And said, 'Fifty pounds.'

One hell of a cut, still too high in Jack's mind, but it was pointless offering nothing as he'd like to.

The man sucked his lip, then said, 'I like you, Jack. You're a hard worker, unlike that layabout.' He flapped a hand towards Mike on the patio. Then added, 'One fifty.'

Jack had become a calculating machine. There was the mortgage, insurance coming up, the van had to go in for its MOT, and he was having to pay good money just to put his scaffolding tower on solid ground. The man was waiting, hands on his waist. Jack was sure the haggling was homing in on a hundred. But it wouldn't do for him to say the figure as Feliks would simply up it.

'Seventy five,' said Jack.

'A hundred and I help you put the scaffolding tower up and take it down.'

Jack thought for a few seconds, sighed and said, 'A deal.'

They shook on it.

Chapter 2

Jack and Feliks took out four fence boards, which simply slotted out of the concrete posts. It was a matter of a few minutes to do them all. And Jack realised that Feliks would perhaps have more work than he had bargained for. For the tower, in its progress along the wall, would have to be taken down to get past each post, and then reassembled the other side of it. Likely every day or two.

The fence boards were laid against the side of Feliks's house. Jack was watching him for he seemed troubled, figuring that Feliks too had realised this wasn't just a once and for all assembly of the tower. He wondered, too, whether the Pole would stick to his side of the bargain.

Jack donned his helmet; Feliks said he didn't need one. And together they set to assembling the scaffolding tower, starting with the two sides, both about a metre and a half high with wheels, connecting them with cross pieces to make the basic square that everything was built up from. They slotted in the next section and stabilised that with bracing poles. When assembled correctly, a built in ladder went up one side as sections were added.

At just over head height, boards were laid internally, but before continuing upwards, they fitted the external braces. These poles stabilised the tower at ground level, rather like guy ropes. Satisfied, Jack went through the trapdoor in the boards. He sat on the planks, legs through the door. The proper procedure for safety's sake, for there should be no standing up until there were sides on a section. Feliks passed up the sides with Jack still sitting. Jack put them in, then stood up. Feliks passed him the braces. And so they went on, up level by level, laying the boards, going through the trap door to put on the sides, standing up and adding the braces each time before going upwards.

In a quarter of an hour they were standing in the two metre square that was the top of the tower. At this level, the highest course of bricks was at Jack's shoulder. The top safety rail, all the way round, was over a metre high. Feliks was leaning on it, looking across at the gardens and their connecting fences, at the variety of lawns, the sheds, the vegetable patches, the last of the summer flowers, the patios and their garden furniture.

'You can see everything up here,' he said with a sly grin. 'I'd better be careful what I do.'

'I don't like working so high,' said Jack. 'It's safe, but feels shaky. I'll be glad when I'm down a level.'

'How you getting your water and mortar up?'

'I've a block and tackle in the van,' said Jack. 'Won't be needing it today. I'll just be chipping out the old mortar. Start the pointing tomorrow.'

Feliks let out a laugh and nudged Jack, indicating a youngish woman on a bicycle who had drawn up. She wheeled her bicycle through the gate. She looked up at Feliks and waved, then almost disappeared from view as she wheeled her bike below them, through the tower, leaving the bike against the wall and continuing herself to the garden. She was wearing a blue cycle helmet over dark brown hair tied back in a ponytail. She had a full figure and was wearing jeans and a T-shirt.

'The cleaner,' said Feliks still smirking. 'Only she doesn't just clean.'

'How do you know?'

'Because they need a babysitter when they go upstairs for a quickie, but it won't be me today as I've got to get on laying the concrete.' Feliks had already begun climbing down the scaffolding tower. 'He'll ask you to do him a favour, I bet you a pound to a penny.'

Jack watched Feliks climb down to ground level. He needed to go down himself to get tools, but didn't want to go down with Feliks. He'd had enough of him. True, Feliks had helped him take out the fencing and put up the scaffolding – but at the loss of a hundred quid. The man was too sharp to be a mate.

He gave him a minute to get clear and then climbed down himself, checking the poles and joints as he went down. You had to be safety conscious on these rigs. He'd heard of towers toppling, usually through carelessness. The external braces not done up properly, wheels not locked, that sort of thing. He knew to check first thing, morning and afternoon.

At ground level, he saw the bike resting against the wall, only a yard up from the tower. Better get that moved. On the handlebars was a canvas bag. She must've forgotten it. It would get covered in his chippings once he started cleaning out the old mortar. He'd have to tell the cleaner. Or could he just move it for her?

As if she'd heard him, she rounded the corner from the patio, holding her helmet.

'I forgot my bag,' she said. 'Full of my mystical sprays.' She gave him a secret smile.

She was shapely, with strong arms and chunky thighs. Not your typical cleaner at all, he thought. Not that he knew much about cleaners. He could imagine her throwing furniture about, and Mike too. Lucky man.

'You'll have to move your bike,' he said. 'I'll be chipping out mortar up top in a few minutes.'

'I'll put it on the patio,' she said, taking the handlebars and starting to wheel the bike.

'I'd better have a word with Mike,' he said. 'Keep everyone out of this alley.'

He followed her, eyeing her figure as she walked, thinking: the best ones go quick. No surprise there. He should keep his mind on work, but it'd been a long time.

Not that he was one for shouting crude comments off scaffolding, but it didn't stop his thoughts.

She propped her bike on the patio, steadying it against the house wall.

She turned to him. 'You here long?'

'Six weeks maybe.' He indicated the walls of the house. 'There's a lot of bricks.'

'I'm Mandy,' she said, holding out her hand. 'I come in twice a week.'

He took her hand. Did she hold it there a little long, or was that wishful thinking?

'Do you live far?' he said.

She shook her head, her ponytail waving on her shoulder. 'Less than five minutes on the bike. Water Lane, Stratford. Do you know it?'

'Yes. I only live round the corner. Earlham Grove.'

'Do you need a cleaner?'

Jack gave a laugh. 'I do. But when you see my place... I don't think you'd want the job.'

'I'm sure I could give you a good spruce up.'

'Rubber gloves and apron?' he said.

'I could fit you in,' she said. 'Except I'm busy at the moment.' She indicated the house. 'But who knows what might happen?'

'Jobs come, jobs go.'

'Don't they just,' she said, and went in through the open French windows.

Mike was inside sitting on the sofa with Lily. He rose when he saw Jack.

'Just the man I wanted to speak to.'

Jack had been warned what was coming. And he wasn't wrong.

'I need a babysitter for half an hour. Can you do me a favour?'

Man to man, such an appeal. Mike had a winning smile,

but really, Jack couldn't be bothered with this.

He said, 'I'm a builder. I've got to get on with the pointing. That's what I get paid for.'

'Please, Jack,' said Mandy.

She and Mike were holding hands. They were leaning in to each other.

No way, thought Jack. I don't want to get involved.

'How much do you earn an hour?' said Mike.

Jack looked at him puzzled. 'Twenty quid if I'm lucky... Why?'

Mike had already pulled out a note. 'Here's a tenner.' He thrust it in Jack's overall pocket. 'Have an early tea break. Make yourself some toast. There's some bacon in the fridge. Have a bacon sandwich.'

'I shouldn't...'

'Go on, mate. Do me a favour.' Mike winked.

'Just take a break,' wheedled Mandy. 'A slow coffee, a bite to eat, and keep an eye on Lily. It's not a lot to ask.'

This was so awkward. Sure, he'd like a handy babysitter in the same position. But he was working for the wife as well as the husband. He was a builder for heaven's sake.

'I can't,' he said. 'Sorry.'

But Mike and Mandy were already striding out of the room. 'Half an hour. Max,' he called. And they were out into the hallway and running up the stairs.

'Hey, Mike! Come back,' he called.

But there was no coming back. There were rapid footsteps in the hall above his head. They weren't hanging about. A door banging shut. They had a tight timetable. It had gone quiet upstairs, but easy to imagine what was happening. Zips and buttons, lips and fingers... Should he go up there and hammer on the door? 'I'm a builder, not a bordello madam!'

And then he relaxed. What the hell. Only half an hour. He'd time them.

Jack sat on the arm of the sofa and watched Lily on the carpet. She was an easy kid, playing a game with a few dolls and stuffed animals that she had placed round some brick blocks. He was still in two minds. By rights, he should run upstairs and order them to get dressed – this is not my work. I am here to point a wall, full stop. Otherwise, he'd be asked to do it every time. He knew the way it would go. One day for certain, he'd have to say no, and mean it. Because the longer it went on, the more that would be resented.

Couldn't they find some other time to screw? Or maybe they did.

Leave them to it. He'd given in. He'd have his slow coffee. Make toast. Early tea break as Mike had said, but he certainly wouldn't do it tomorrow.

But to make tea and toast, he had to get Lily into the kitchen. And he knew from experience with Mia, that when kids are happily playing, you have to leave them. Unless he could enter her game.

'Would your dollies like some food?' he said.

Lily looked at him quizzically. Then pointed out food: dolls' cakes and fruit made of plaster and plastic. A regular dolls' picnic.

'What about a banana?' he said.

Lily rifled through a bucket of bricks and items, and came up triumphantly with a tiny banana.

He was impressed. Maybe she wasn't yet talking, but she knew the words.

'Toast and cheese,' he suggested.

She shook her head vehemently, and went back to placing her guests and their food.

Could he leave her for a minute or two? Go in the kitchen, grab a coffee. Forget bacon sandwiches, but biscuits or a banana. Whatever was cold and easy. Mia as a toddler, he would have just picked up and taken into the kitchen with her dolls, and put up with her protest. But his acquaintance with

Lily was short. Besides which, you can do things with your own kids that you can't do with somebody else's.

For heaven's sake. He should be pointing! Not negotiating with a toddler.

He strode into the kitchen. There was a half-filled coffee pot, pretty warm. He made a cup quickly and searched shelves and tins. And came out with coffee and half a dozen biscuits on a plate.

Jack sat on the sofa and stretched out his boots, the biscuits on the arm. He drank and dipped biscuits. The cement mixer was chugging in the next door garden. That money-grubbing bastard. A hundred quid for damn all! There was bumping on the ceiling. The light was swinging in a pendulum curve.

Going at it.

He watched the child on the carpet, happy enough, not an inkling that her parents' marriage was in danger. This couldn't go on, kid. They were so careless, they didn't care.

He'd done many things as a builder that weren't strictly building work, but never babysitting. A first time for everything. But next time, he must refuse. Make it clear when he saw them again.

Customers always made demands. Mostly about noise and mess; make less. Keep plaster off the carpet and piano. Or they'd changed their mind when you were halfway through. The pendulum light was hypnotic. He wouldn't do this again. He would insist.

His phone rang.

Jack took it out of his pocket. Alison, his ex. What did she want? Something annoying to be sure. But at least it took his mind off what was happening above.

'Hello, Alison. How's it going?'

'Awful,' she said. 'This school is the pits. They don't know how to do anything. I might as well have a zombie for a deputy...'

He stopped listening as she began going on about Ofsted, governors and site supervisors.

'So can you?' she said.

'What?'

'Look after Mia tonight.'

He shook himself into listening mode. She'd got off complaining and was speaking to him again.

The front door shut. Who could that be?

'OK,' he said. 'I'm at home tonight.'

Jean came into the room. She stopped and looked at him, arms akimbo.

'What the hell are you doing?'

For a few seconds, he couldn't speak with a mouthful of biscuit. She was as neat and as professional as when she'd left earlier. And twice as intimidating. He closed the phone call; he'd have to explain to Alison later.

'I'm just having a coffee break,' he said warily, 'and looking after Lily for a minute or two.'

'And I thought you were a builder,' she exclaimed, as if about to strike him. 'Not an au pair.'

'Mike invited me in for a coffee, while he...' he began.

'What?'

What was he to say? There was no right answer. Only a variety of wrong ones. He grabbed at the nearest.

'He had to talk to someone. Business. A gig coming up...'

'I bet there is.'

She dropped her briefcase on an armchair and headed out of the room, turning for an instant at the door:

'I'll talk to you when I get back.'

He wanted to say, shouldn't you be here looking after your child – but there was no one to say it to. She'd flown out of the room. There was going to be a scene. Which would far outweigh any sharp words she had for him. Maybe she'd forget him. Jack listened. He couldn't hear her on the stairs of the landing. No doubt, she was creeping up, probably carrying her shoes.

Any minute there'd be fireworks.

Jack drank his coffee, savouring the few seconds of quietness. Lily was playing happily. His daughter Mia would be coming over after school. That was fine. He had no thoughts of booze when she was around. Responsibility took over. And wasn't there a conjunction of Venus and Jupiter this evening? He'd noted it from his astronomy magazine. About 7.30 pm, just after sunset. They could go over and see it on Wanstead Flats.

There was yelling from upstairs. The riot had begun. Her voice. Screaming, the cleaner probably. He couldn't hear Mike. Though what did he have to say, really? Caught, most likely naked, her legs round his neck. This was the quiet space, out of the action, though it did spring to mind that he might not have a job when the hullabaloo settled.

A door banged, the volume of the yelling crescendoed. He caught the odd words: 'divorce', 'whore', 'lazy bastard'. Sufficient to give the flavour. He wished he was on top of his tower pointing. More screaming and door banging.

Lily had grabbed his arm and was looking upward. She was holding a teddy.

He'd quite forgotten the toddler playing on the carpet. As a responsible adult he should close the sitting room door. Except it was rather late now. Besides, he wasn't that responsible when it came down to it. Both parents had pressed him into childminding for want of somebody better.

He said, 'Humpty Dumpty sat on a wall, Humpty Dumpty had a great fall...' keeping the nursery rhyme slow as if there were no noises off stage. And then followed with *Mary, Mary, Quite contrary...* thinking how apt the nursery rhymes were.

He'd just begun *Little Jack Horner* when there was

running down the stairs and shrieking. Something thrown, a shoe, he guessed. He caught a glimpse of someone half dressed, one bare foot, passing the door. And wondered again whether he was about to be dismissed. He had their deposit at least. That would see him about even. Not his plan, but he was no longer in charge.

He was on *Hey Diddle Diddle* as Jean entered the room, her face a storm.

She yelled, 'It's not your place to babysit so my husband can shag the cleaner.'

Jack took a deep breath and began his excuses, hoping he could get himself off the hook.

'I didn't know he'd be doing that.' A lie of course. He continued. 'I came in to tell Mike that I'd be chipping out the old mortar by the side of the house and not to go that way.' A truthful bit. 'He told me to have a coffee and keep an eye on Lily while he made a couple of calls.'

'Are you CRB checked – or whatever it's called these days?'

Jack knew vaguely what CRB was, police checked for any history of child abuse.

'I've got a 13 year old daughter,' he said.

'Who you might abuse every night for all I know.'

'How dare you!' he threw back at her, then stopped himself. 'I shouldn't be here, looking after your daughter. I didn't want to be. Get it? Your husband just abandoned me. I had no idea what was going on.' The same lie, but he had a job to protect, and from the look on her face, things might be going his way. 'He said five minutes, no longer. He told me he was going to make phone calls. I should have a coffee...' He stood up. Lily was pulling at his arm, trying to drag him down on the sofa once more.

'I'd best get back to work,' he said, hoping this was it and she'd run out of steam.

'I'm sorry,' she began, and then was weeping. 'It's not

your fault but...' she said between sniffs, 'I don't know whether we want a builder or not. Considering what's going on.' Then added, wiping her eyes with the back of her hand, 'Unless for our marriage.'

'I heard the word divorce,' he said carefully.

'You heard correctly,' she said. She flapped her hands. 'I suspected something. Perfume on his shirt. And I thought, the cleaner. Who else? I saw the way he looked at her and she at him. So I pretended I had an appointment this morning, allowed them just about long enough...' She gave a half laugh. 'I really walloped the woman. Pulled her hair. What a savage I was. It's such a betrayal of everything.'

Mike came in, hair tousled, subdued.

'Jean...'

'I'm leaving,' said Jack rising and holding up his hands. 'I know the two of you have things to say. All I want to know is whether you want me to carry on.'

'I don't know,' she said, and turned to her husband. 'What do you think, Mike?'

'It needs doing,' he said weakly.

'Yes,' she said, blowing a raspberry. 'It needs doing. We can agree on something at least. And whether we sell the house or stay, it needs doing. Sorry we've put you to so much trouble, Jack. Please carry on.'

'I'll get back to work then,' he said, and headed for the French windows.

'Sorry, mate,' Mike called after him as he stepped on to the patio.

Chapter 3

Trevor rang the bell again, and waited half a minute. When no one came, he rang it continuously. He could hear it resounding through the flat. There was no doubt the bell was working. His mother was a little hard of hearing, but surely she would hear that? She always did other times. He gave up after a minute and considered what he should do. There were flyers poking out of the letter box. He took them out. Pizza, a letting agency, vouchers for the Co-op, extra tuition. Plus a letter, official looking.

He sat on her window sill, undecided. A middle aged black man, hair greying, a little portly, wearing a brown suit, a white shirt and a tie. He'd come that morning from Southend, leaving his wife and son to run their hardware shop, when his mother hadn't been answering her phone for more than a day. Taken the train to Stratford, then he'd changed to catch another for the two stops to Forest Gate; the way he normally came when visiting his mother. Much easier than driving when they lived only five minutes from Southend Victoria station.

Why wasn't she answering? He could think of no good reasons for the silence. She might have collapsed or even be dead. At 82, not in the best of health, and forgetful. He'd feared such an outcome. She'd lived in this basement flat for over 30 years. His father had had his heart attack here ten years ago – and died in the ambulance on the way to hospital.

She'd said that he should have a key, and it would have been easy enough to get her key cut. Just go up the road to the high street. He was always going to do it, one of those minor, not very important jobs you could always postpone.

No point thinking of what he should have done, Millie would remind him well enough. He would have to talk to his mother's neighbours. But he was a shy man, finding it difficult to talk to strangers. He could do it in the shop, talk of wood and drills, of screw sizes and PVA glue. Easy when a customer wanted something and so began the conversation. But with strangers – you have to start. Small talk. He didn't know how to do it. Practical things he could manage, churchy things, family things. So much better when they asked you first. Usually he left it to his wife to do the talking, except she wasn't here – and he simply couldn't go back to Southend without knowing. He'd only have to come back again. And Millie would go on and on. Quite rightly, he had to admit.

He rang the bell once more, knowing it was pointless, his ear to the letter box. He stopped ringing and peered through the flap. No sign of life in the hallway. The front door glass was frosted, no hope of seeing anything through that. Trevor had already tried looking through the window of her front room, but the room was gloomy and he couldn't see a thing through the full-length net curtains. His mother had a horror at being peered at. Though who on earth could see anything from up there, when it was eight steps down to her front door?

There was nothing for it; he'd have to speak to the neighbours. It couldn't be avoided. There was that Polish man, the landlord. His mother wasn't keen on him. Said he didn't like her being a secure tenant and was reluctant to do any repairs. His mother had had to complain to *Age UK* to get him to fix a blocked sink. And there was that prostitute in the other flat. She made him uncomfortable. Made him think thoughts he'd rather not think. She was attractive in a plump sort of way. But his horror of what all those men did to her, and she to them, made her hard to look at. His thoughts could be encapsulated in one word, sin. She was sin, she made others sinful. A single look at her reminded him of his own wickedness.

Trevor climbed the stairs to ground level. And stood in the yard looking up at the house, hoping someone would come to his aid. There was no help, he'd have to go to them. He climbed the steps to the front door. There were two bells labelled A and B. He rang the A bell, and the instant he'd done so, thought – Oh, that's the prostitute's flat. But it was done.

Why had he done that? Was it wickedness? A desire to see her. The thought of her made him shudder. He could hear footsteps inside. He straightened up, brushing his perfectly clean trousers down. The door opened and she was before him. Sin in the guise of a youngish, black woman in a red dress with too much bosom showing, shiny, crinkled black hair flowing off her shoulders. She greeted him with a smile, through clean, very white dental work.

She said, 'You're Mrs Jackson's son, aren't you? I've been worried about her.'

'That's why I rang your bell,' he said, rubbing his hands nervously. 'I can't remember your name. I'm sorry.'

'Saffron.'

'Pleased to meet you. I'm Trevor. I've been trying to contact Mum since yesterday morning. And she hasn't answered the phone. She never goes out for more than an hour or two. So I knew there was something wrong and came here first thing. I've been ringing her bell for the last ten minutes.'

Her bosom was very disturbing. You dressed that way perhaps for a party. Not for every day. A reminder of the prostitutes he'd visited before he was married. He despised himself for it; the women who made him want them. His neck was prickly, sweat running down his back.

Saffron said, 'I've got your mother's cat. I had to feed him yesterday and this morning too.'

'Oh, let me give you something...' he fiddled in his trouser pocket.

She held up a hand. 'Please don't bother, Trevor. I like Monty. He gets on with my own cat, Frank. They patrol the garden together. Won't let any other cats in. Monty often comes in through the garden cat-flap for extra food. Except I know it wasn't extra today but all he'd had. I know a starving cat.'

'Thank you for looking after him,' he said. 'I much appreciate that.' He hesitated before continuing. 'But if Monty hasn't been fed, except by you of course, it can only mean...' He couldn't go on. It was too distressing.

'I think we must get into her flat,' said Saffron, putting a hand on his shoulder, making him shudder. 'Feliks might have a key. He's out the back in the garden. Come in. We'll go out and see him.'

Feliks, though, didn't have a key. The cement mixer was groaning as they came down the garden path. He told Trevor he'd never needed a key, she was always in. Trevor explained why he'd come and Feliks caught up quickly.

'We'll have to break in,' he said. 'Let me think of the best way.' He scratched his curly hair. There was cement under his finger nails. 'I think the back door would be easiest. We need a hammer. But my tools are at my other house.' He thought for a second, then said, 'Let's have a word with the builder next door.'

Jack was at the top of the scaffolding tower when they called him down. Quite a flurry of them, he thought, looking down at the group at the bottom of the scaffolding tower beckoning him. For the last hour, he'd been happy to get away from the tensions of the house and simply chip out mortar. Now what? Leaving his pointing tools up top, he climbed down the tower. At ground level it was explained they needed to break in to the basement flat – as it was feared Mrs Jackson might have collapsed in there. And they needed a hammer.

Jack got his toolbox from his van, and the four of them went to the back door of the old lady's flat out in the garden. Jack positioned his safety goggles and put on working gloves.

'Stand back,' he ordered. 'There might be flying glass.'

He swung the hammer at a small window in the back door. It cracked and bits dropped inside. Jack hammered round the outside of the small frame, chipping out the pieces of glass still attached. He put his gloved hand through the window, and felt around.

'There's a key in the lock,' he said. 'See if I can turn it.' He pushed his arm further in. The key was stiff. It was awkward from the outside. Then it turned, and he withdrew his hand.

Feliks twisted the door handle and opened the door, and they followed him into the flat kitchen. It was old fashioned and tidy, all the surfaces wiped down.

'She has a cleaner in every week,' said Trevor. 'The same one they have next door.'

Jack added nothing to that information; it wasn't pertinent. They went into the hall. There were only two other rooms, apart from the bathroom. Cautiously, they entered the sitting room. There was a crucifix in the middle of the mantelpiece and family photos on either side, one a slimmer Trevor, ten years younger. A Radio Times lay open on the sofa.

They trooped out, and crossed the hallway to the bedroom. Another very tidy room, the bed made, her clothing in the wardrobe or the large chest of drawers with its round wooden knobs.

A quick glance in the bathroom and they went back to the sitting room and sat down. Saffron's phone rang. She pulled it out.

'Oops, must go, I've a customer.'

And she left them.

'A busy woman,' said Feliks with a smirk.

'What does she do?' said Jack.

Feliks made a crude gesture and Jack said no more, not altogether surprised. From his platform, he'd noted a number of visitors to the house, all male.

'Where can she be?' exclaimed Trevor. 'I was so sure she'd be here.'

'Her memory was bad,' said Feliks consolingly. 'Perhaps she went somewhere and forgot where she was.'

'She could be in a local hospital,' suggested Jack.

'It's years since I lived round here,' sighed Trevor. 'I wanted her to move out to Southend so we could keep an eye on her. But she said she wouldn't know anyone. She likes her church and her bingo.' He stopped. 'What hospitals are there locally?'

'Newham General is the closest,' said Jack. 'There's Whipps Cross in Leytonstone and...' he thought for a moment and added, 'Maybe London Hospital. If you phone admissions, they'll tell if she's been brought in.'

Trevor opened and closed his hands helplessly. 'I've only got my mobile. And it's not one of those smart phones...'

'Come up to my flat,' offered Feliks, putting a hand on his shoulder. 'We can find the numbers on the internet, and you can phone from there.'

'Thank you so much,' said Trevor.

'The least I can do.'

'I'll get back to work,' said Jack rising.

'And perhaps you can do me a favour,' said Feliks to Jack. 'Board up that window in the back door. I've got the key now.'

Jack was tempted to say – a hundred quid, but instead said, 'OK.'

It was better to be on good terms with Feliks.

Chapter 4

Mandy, in spite of her panic, was able to get her bike from the patio, but she only had on one shoe and one sock. She wheeled the bike out to the pavement and walked it along the street for a while. Then rested the bike against a wall, and took off her single shoe and sock. She put them in her backpack. Twenty five pounds, the trainers had cost her. Dammit. She hoped Mike could get the other shoe back for her. She only had one other pair.

Her face was stinging where Jean had slapped her, head aching where her hair had been pulled back. She was still wet between her legs, as Mike had been in the throes of coming as Jean entered. All in all, a bad day, and she feared it would get worse.

She was due at her next cleaning job, but she'd have to go home first. Clean up, put shoes and socks on. If she were quick, she'd only be half an hour late. Which wouldn't be unusual, as being delayed at Mike's was par for the course. Mandy put on her cycle helmet, reflecting that it would have been useful when Jean arrived, got on her bike and cycled slowly in bare feet.

It had been bound to happen. Surprising that they'd got away with it for as long as they had. They'd grown careless. Difficult not to; you can't have one ear on the door when you are making love. A car came by her and hooted. She was wobbling in the middle of the road. She dismounted and walked the bike on the pavement for a little way. Then cycled on.

There was her relationship with Mike to sort out. Where was it going? Jean had been screaming 'divorce' – so maybe there was a future. She'd known Mike ever since they'd worked together in *Liverpool Lullaby*. Years ago, way before she was their cleaner, they'd had a scene, with Mike claiming he was jamming with mates when he arrived home in the early hours. He needed to wind down, he would tell Jean.

Mandy halted at the Atherton Road junction, and slowly cycled round to the right. A man had stopped to stare at her, her slowness, her bright red toenails. Not quite Lady Godiva. She was hot, her face burning. She must get that shoe back. She couldn't afford another pair. A dribble was running down her leg; blood, or more intimate liquids? She must get off the street. Get respectable.

It had been so quick. What – ten minutes ago? Mike gasping on top of her in the throes of lovemaking, and then Jean screaming and on her like a tornado, scratching and hitting. That clump round the face had knocked her against the wall. Could she sue?

Hardly.

She drew up at her house; she had a ground floor flat on Water Lane, Stratford. A housing association property; she'd been lucky to get it. She leaned her bike on the wall dividing her house from the next, wriggled her shoulders and picked stones out of the soles of her feet. Heaven knows how she'd carry on cleaning today. But she had to.

Have a quick shower, freshen up. She opened her door, and brought her bike into the hallway. She must leave what had happened behind and get into work mode. Be an actor. Her part was the cleaner. Method act. Be it. Smile it. Give ready platitudes about the weather. Talk about Coronation Street.

Her phone rang.

She looked at the number. It was her cleaning agency. A cancellation perhaps. Or more work?

'Hello,' she said tentatively. 'I'm just heading off to 92 Romford Road.'

'Mandy,' said her boss. 'I've just had a call from Mrs Lucas.'

She had to think for a second who Mrs Lucas was. Of course. Her.

'And unless you have anything to say to the contrary, I am sacking you for gross misconduct.'

'What did she say to you?'

'That she caught you and her husband in bed. Is that true?'

She thought for a second. Could she possibly deny it? Brazen it out. Oh, to hell with it! She hated cleaning, being the menial of the menial.

'Yes,' she said.

'Was it consensual?'

'Yes.'

'Then you are fired as of this minute. I am sorry, Mandy. But we can't have this. We are not an escort agency. We have a reputation. I have assured Mrs Lucas that I will deal with this immediately – and I shall get back to her and tell her you have been sacked.'

'And you'll give me a lousy reference, I suppose?'

'I wouldn't apply to us, Mandy. I would have to say why you were dismissed. We will pay you up to date. And that is that. I am sorry, Mandy. Clients liked you. But this is beyond the pale. Goodbye.'

And the call closed.

She sank onto the sofa. She was in no hurry now. No job to rush off to. She could hardly argue with what had just happened. Or could she? Suppose she had called Jean a liar. Mike would have to call his wife a liar too. Mandy would likely be suspended, pending investigation. And she'd have to lie on paper, lie to a tribunal, and get found out in the end. Jean would most likely sue her. Though she wouldn't get anything as she didn't have anything. She could imagine Jean having the sheets analysed for her DNA. And my heavens, her knickers were there too? No chance.

She laughed. You can't argue against knickers.

Maybe sacking was a better finale. But did it end there? With that phone call... Would she get Job Seekers Allowance?

She went on-line and asked Google – can I get JSA if I have been sacked? Google gave her variations on the theme of No. She would be sanctioned, which meant no money. And that could be for three months or as long as six. She could appeal, but to appeal she would need grounds.

And she had none. Not with her knickers as prime evidence.

Chapter 5

Jack stretched his arms and rolled his shoulders. He looked over the half a dozen courses below the eaves that he'd chipped out. He'd gone as far as he could reach in either direction from the tower. Lunch. This afternoon, he'd point them with fresh mortar. That'd be his way of working; chip out decayed mortar to a couple of centimetres for a number of courses and then point them as he went along.

Good to be up top and away, after the fuss earlier. He'd been press ganged into childminding, and almost got himself in line for a sacking. Then he'd just about started work and there was the old lady's flat to break into. That was an interruption more than anything else. He'd never met her. Felt sorry for her son as they went round her flat, but it was only a slight involvement. He'd simply hoped Trevor could track his mother down, and forgotten the affair.

It had taken ages to get going this morning. Often the way. But the scaffolding tower was assembled, even if it meant paying off Feliks, and the first courses chipped out. He'd got used to being high up, forgotten almost. The work was simple, a little boring he might say, but the sunshine and height left him to his own thoughts. He hoped the weather would hold out. You never could tell with late September.

Work made him feel useful. Superior even, up here, above the squabbles, a watcher of human affairs. Involved in the closeness of the work, that stubborn bit of mortar to be chiselled out, forgetting even about sex, thinking at one point about the conjunction of the planets this evening, how it came about, how often it might occur. And glancing at passers-by below, those damned sinners on the street.

Lunch.

He glanced at his hands; they were lined in grit, the nails full of mortar. He should wash, but didn't want to go into the house; not knowing the reception he'd get. Mike was in disgrace so it wouldn't do to befriend him. She had a hell of a temper, even though she'd apologised, but could easily have another go at him. And there was no arguing with the facts, without him it wouldn't have happened. With him babysitting, they could go upstairs and set the light swinging.

So, stay out of the way. Then he wouldn't have to explain or lie to anyone. Wash under the yard tap and eat in his van.

But first he needed to put something right. Jack sat down on the boards and took out his phone. He looked at his watch; she'd be on her lunch hour now.

'Hello, Jack,' said Alison.

'Sorry about cutting you off earlier,' he said.

'I heard a very angry woman. What were you doing?'

'I was looking after her child.'

'Who should've been?'

'Her husband.'

'What was he up to?'

'He was in bed with the cleaner.'

Alison had a long chuckle. 'Were you keeping watch?'

'I certainly wasn't.'

'You must have had some part in it.'

'Hardly,' he said uncomfortably.

'I don't believe you. I deal with liars all day long.'

'He dumped the kid on me,' he insisted. 'What was I supposed to do?'

'Chase after him. Give the kid back.'

'You're right. I'm wrong. As usual. It's just that...' He was seeing himself drinking coffee, watching Lily on the carpet. It had happened so quickly. He hadn't wanted a row. And there was the child to consider.

'You men,' snapped Alison. 'It's what you'd have wanted him to do for you.'

He was silent for a few seconds. 'I hope not,' he said weakly, then added, 'Their marriage is bust anyway. But you're right, I should've kept out of it.'

'Best thing,' she said. 'What's in it for you?'

'It's not so easy, Ali. I have to keep on their right side. They *are* employing me.'

'Oh yes? A guy helping a guy. And looking for excuses.'

Alison's sarcasm, mild as it was, went to the heart of it.

'I won't do it again,' he said contritely. Something he'd told himself several times over the morning.

'Good. And to change the subject, you're alright for Mia at your place tonight?'

'Yep. Fine,' he said, relieved to be off the hook. 'You got a date?'

'Yes, I have. I'm trying computer dating. And I tell you, it's so nerve-wracking. Meeting a complete stranger, admitting you're lonely. I have to keep saying to myself I'm not a bad catch, not quite past it. Good salary, respectable.'

'Depends what you're looking for.'

'More than a one night stand. A relationship. Remember those things?'

'I've read about them. They're rumoured to be a good thing.'

She sighed. 'I hope he's not another liar.'

'Back on the old theme.'

'Sex makes everyone a liar,' she said thoughtfully. 'No one's innocent.'

'Not even you?'

'Not even me, I am loath to admit. To you especially. Dressing up, make-up, high heeled shoes, pushing truth so far it's almost off the edge.'

'You're a philosopher.'

'Of life and love and school staffing. Bye.'

She rang off. He took a deep breath, glad that had gone off without too much rancour. It had begun uncomfortably but got more chatty. She'd even admitted that she wasn't perfect. He should've taped it for future use.

Lunch.

He left his tools at the top of the tower. They were safe enough behind the foot boards. He climbed down the ladder. At the bottom, he left his goggles and hard hat on the lowest boards, which were just over head height. He went into the garden to give his hands a rinse under the outside tap, prior to eating in the van, out of the way of arguing couples.

He came out to the patio, where Jean was seated at the table with her laptop. Jack almost stepped back into the alley, but she looked up as he came out.

'Just need to rinse my hands for lunch,' he said, indicating the tap on the wall of the house.

She nodded. 'Do you want a coffee?'

He thought for a second or two. The woman could be feral, but it seemed a conciliatory offer. And she was the boss. The one who paid him. He'd learnt that much.

'Sure.'

'Bring your lunch out here,' she said. 'I'll make us some coffee.'

She went inside. Jack rinsed his hands under the tap, and flapped them in the air to get the drips off as he went out to get his lunch from the van. He had noted that the bike had gone. The cleaner must've cycled off with one shoe. That was a screaming match. Maybe he should have his lunch alone. Keep out of trouble. But he'd been on his own long enough this morning. Mrs Lucas was attractive, she was company. And he hoped to be working here a while. Though he did wonder where Mike was. Dead in the bedroom perhaps.

Best behaviour. Don't mention the war.

He sat down at the table, and opened his lunch box.

Hardly needed a box for what was in it. Two cheese sandwiches. There hadn't been much else in the house.

In the next door garden, the cement mixer was chugging on. Busy fellow, Feliks. That's how you get rich. He was reminded that he still had to repair that window in the back door. He wondered what had happened to the old lady. They'd probably find her in one of the local hospitals. A fall, a heart attack. It happens to us all. He'd best do the repair before he did anything else this afternoon, as Feliks was an awkward so and so.

She was taking her time with the coffee. Maybe making phone calls. Telling her best friend about Mike and his goings on. Jack could sympathise with Mike, stuck at home looking after an infant. Life needs its high points or it's tedium, with nothing on the horizon but more tedium. So Mike shags the cleaner. A hell of a risk, but a break from routine for an unemployed musician.

Keep that to yourself.

Jack took a sandwich and began eating, knowing he had that tendency himself, the fear of the sameness of things. It had got him into drinking a few years ago. *In Vino Veritas* was a stupid saying. A marketing mantra from vineyard owners. There was no truth at all in a bottle of plonk, rather an escape from the verities, the quickest road out of London as someone at Alcohol Halt had said.

And a rough ride back.

Jean came out carrying a tray. It held two coffees, biscuits, but also some salad in a bowl and a couple of forks.

'I thought your lunch might be a bit plain,' she said placing the tray on the table.

'Don't spoil me,' he said. 'I'm here for six weeks.' He picked out a cherry tomato. It was sweet and juicy. He went for another and noted she was not eating.

She saw him looking. 'I'm not hungry,' she said. 'More than filled up with anger.'

'Where's Mike?' he asked carefully.

'He's taking Lily to West Ham Park. And he can stay there for all I care.'

She was angry alright. He could feel the heat across the table.

'I have an appointment with my solicitor this afternoon. I've had enough of him. It's one thing keeping him. Well, someone has to look after Lily. But to find him in bed with the cleaner...' She waved her hands furiously. 'No, no.'

He said nothing. This was dangerous ground. Wherever you stepped you would sink.

'I don't know how long it's been going on for,' she continued. 'But he had the cheek to tell me it was the first time. And that is such a stupid lie. It's so obvious she didn't do much cleaning, but I put up with it. Put up with his weed smoking... But now it's at an end. I'm making good money, I can buy childcare without the complications of a drug-smoking shagger.'

'What do you do?'

Mike had already told him, but he'd forgotten almost at once as he only half understood.

'I'm an author entrepreneur,' she said.

He looked at her blankly. 'Sorry. It's not my field.'

She laughed. 'I assume everyone knows. Just shows the small circles I move in. I write suspense fantasy. Fairy stories for grown ups, I call them. With sex, torture, sword fighting, and magic. I chop someone's head off whenever the excitement flags. I self publish them as e-books, and then I do all that I can to market them. I maintain my fan list, I run courses on Skype, I blog every week, send out a newsletter.' She stopped and added, 'Do you want to be on my list?'

'I don't know,' he said, nonplussed at the request.

'What was the last book you read?'

He had to think for a moment, caught out by the

question. Then said, 'A month or two back. *The Universe Revealed.*'

'Ah, sci fi,' she said. 'Future dystopian or biblical apocalypse?'

'Actually, not fiction. About the stars and planets. My daughter gave it to me as a Christmas present. Great pictures of the planets and nebulae.' He gestured as if half ashamed. 'I'm interested in that stuff. Got a telescope.'

'Strange for a builder.'

'Why?'

'I'd have thought builders just head for the pub, get drunk, swear all the time, beat up their wives...'

'I never beat up my wife.' Then he added lightly, 'She kicked me out for other reasons.'

'So the rest of the cliché is true.'

'Drink was a problem,' he admitted. God, that was downplaying it. 'Talking of books, I used to like Ian Rankin,' he said, to change tack. 'That Scottish writer and Rebus, his detective, a bit of a maverick, I read a lot of his stuff. Until I went on the wagon – then I couldn't read them anymore. Rebus drinks non stop, hardly a page when he didn't have a pint or a whisky in his hand. You don't want to read about that when you've gone TT.'

'So maybe you could try some suspense fantasy?'

'Hobbits are not my thing.'

'I'm insulted, Jack,' she said in mock affront. 'Tolkien couldn't write women characters to save his life. There's not a sniff of sex in Middle Earth. Heaven knows how they reproduced. Try one of mine for a change.'

'Alright.' It would have been rude to say anything else. But whether he'd actually read it...

'I'll send you an e-copy. Your email address is on your estimate. Do have some more salad.'

Jack took a couple of spring onions, another cherry tomato and a piece of celery.

He said boldly, 'I'll read your book, if you watch the conjunction of Venus and Jupiter with me tonight.'

She laughed, then shook her head. 'I mustn't. I can't be in bed with the builder if I'm bemoaning my husband screwing the cleaner.'

'I meant really look at the planets,' he said, slightly offended. 'Over Wanstead Flats. About seven thirty. There really is a conjunction. My daughter will be with us, anyway.'

'Won't she resent me coming?'

'Not if I let her read a bit of your book,' he said, thinking on the hoof, which always had its dangers. 'She reads fantasy, mostly vampire stuff, but your books sound like her sort.'

'Mine's a bit raunchy for a 13 year old.'

'She tells me she reads some real steamy stuff.'

Jean shrugged. 'You're the parent. And OK, I'll come over the flats with you. But nothing more. Just for an hour or so. I've got to prepare a video talk tonight.'

The front door slammed in the house.

'Oh my god, he's back,' she exclaimed, throwing her hands up. 'I don't know how we're going to live together after that fiasco. I'd like to kick him out but we bought this place together.' She leaned across the table and said quietly, 'Will you stay a little longer to fend off a row?'

Exactly what Alison had warned him against. But he still had half a sandwich, some coffee and odd bits of salad on his plate.

Mike came out, holding Lily by the hand.

'Did you like the park, sweetheart?' said Jean picking up Lily and seating her on her lap.

Protection, thought Jack. The child beamed.

Mike was leaning by the French windows as if unsure whether to stay outside or go in.

'How's it going, Jack?' he said.

'I've chiselled out half a dozen courses. I'm going to point them this afternoon.'

'Good for you. Take advantage of the weather. Lovely in the park.' He turned to his wife. 'I've got to go out this afternoon.'

'Where?'

He shrugged. 'Just out.'

Jack saw Jean bite her lip. He was sure they'd have a real dingdong but for his presence. They'd probably got used to ignoring Lily. Were they really going to stay together like this?

'You'll have to look after Lily,' said Mike.

'I'm going out too,' she said stiffly.

'Then you'll have to take her with.' And he stepped back into the house.

Jean was grinding her teeth, hands clawed as if to scratch at his cheeks. But he was gone.

'How on earth can I do any work in this atmosphere?' she exclaimed. She gave Lily a small tomato that the toddler played with like a marble, rolling it in her hands. 'I bet he's going to see his bitch.' She closed her eyes for a second, then added, 'I got her sacked, you know. I'm not paying for her to come here and mess up my marriage.'

'Understandable,' said Jack neutrally.

'Maybe he'll move in with her,' she mused. 'Best thing all round. Maybe I shouldn't have got her sacked, but I was so angry.'

'I heard some of it,' said Jack.

'I lash out at everyone when I'm in a strop,' she said, and turned to her daughter. 'We're going up to Stratford soon, Lily. Would you like that?'

Lily nodded.

'Why won't you talk, dearest?' She turned to Jack. 'She understands so much, but she just won't talk. My mother goes on and on about it.' She imitated, 'Nearly three and not talking. You should take her to a psychiatrist.' She bent down to Lily and kissed the top of her head. 'There's nothing wrong with you, darling.'

'I wasn't talking until I was three and a half,' said Jack.

'There you are, sweetie,' said Jean with a laugh, 'you might end up a builder!'

Chapter 6

Trevor was in Feliks' lounge, laptop and phone on the pine table. The furniture in the room was a mixture, much of it picked up from evicted tenants. Feliks would take his pick at such times, jettisoning older for newer when opportunities occurred. Each item, he could point out who it had belonged to and when. He had a keen memory for such events. The sofa for instance, that came from a Pakistani couple with four kids who had done a runner. The table and chairs from two Latvian girls who were baristas in Starbucks and attempted to live the high life on a lowlife income. And the 50 inch flat screen TV from an old woman on benefits who had six cats defecating and peeing at will. When she died, her flat needed an ultra clean which Feliks resented every time he switched on the TV. Even the computer was loot. It had belonged to an Iranian student doing a PhD at some London college. Sue me, Feliks had said to him. And even got a hundred quid off him, so the student could copy his thesis onto a memory stick from the laptop which Feliks kept.

He and Trevor had spent over an hour contacting local hospitals. First finding the phone numbers from the internet, then phoning and checking whether Trevor's mother was there. Feliks was impatient, while Trevor became more distraught at each negative reply.

'Not at Newham General,' he said, 'Not at Whipps Cross or the Royal London. Where else is there?'

'I think that's enough,' said Feliks. He wanted to eat, but didn't see why he should feed Trevor.

'What's that one in Hackney?' Trevor scratched his head. 'It used to be called Hackney Hospital... then changed its name. I can't remember to what. I haven't lived round here in years.'

Feliks rolled his eyes and typed Hackney Hospital into Google. The answer came up at once. Hackney Hospital had closed in 1995, and was replaced by Homerton Hospital. Feliks went into the site and found the number for new admissions. He wrote it on a scrap of paper and passed it to Trevor. The fourth one he'd done that way.

Watching him phone was like watching a man having his fingernails pulled out. But Feliks wasn't going to do it for him. Wasn't it enough having him up here in the first place? He regretted having offered.

Trevor had to psych himself up for each call. He couldn't simply do it, but had to breathe deeply, count to ten and say a little prayer, or something like. Then he would pounce on the phone and punch out the numbers before he could stop himself. He found it agony talking to strangers, explaining what he wanted, waiting for them, each time expecting to be reprimanded. Any other situation he would have given up ages ago, passed on the chore to Millie. But suppose his mother was in hospital, at death's door even?

He at last phoned Homerton, asked for admissions, held the phone and waited, eyes closed, dreading the voice to come. Admissions replied, and necessity caused him to speak, falteringly. He told them his mother might have come in yesterday or even the day before. Too hasty in his confusion, further information had to be elicited before the telephonist could assist. But eventually he came up with the name, date of birth, racial category and when she might have come in. Enough for another wait, and for another negative.

Trevor put down the phone, trembling, as if awaiting execution by firing squad. Feliks was exasperated. The calls could have been made in quarter of an hour. What a performance! Each one a muddle as if he hadn't made the last and didn't know what was required.

45

'Suppose one of the hospitals has made a mistake?' said Trevor in panic. 'And she's really there but they have her details wrong.'

Feliks threw up his hands. The man was driving him crazy.

He said, 'Then you'll just have to go and visit them all.'

'How will that help?' exclaimed Trevor. 'If they've got her name wrong or whatever – how will I know she's there?'

Feliks rose and turned his back on Trevor, going to his window. He wished the silly man would leave. He'd allowed him to phone four hospitals. That was already more than enough. He himself should be out there, in the garden, working on his shed. He could just make out the cement mixer from here, between the straggly beanpoles of the vegetable patch. The cement he'd laid would already be setting in the shuttering; he must take advantage of this good weather. It could rain for the next fortnight. He didn't want to keep the mixer a day too long. Why pay hire charges when you don't have to?

'There's a hospital in Goodmayes,' exclaimed Trevor. 'I can't remember its name. Up Barley Lane. I remember I had an auntie in there. What's it called? And there's one in Romford...'

'And one in Berlin,' said Feliks.

Trevor looked at him, and got the message.

'I am sorry,' he said, wiping his brow with his handkerchief. 'I have taken up so much of your time.'

Feliks showed his empty hands. 'She is my tenant. But you can only do so much. I would like to find her as much as you... but there has to be a limit.'

'What should I do?'

Feliks shrugged. 'Wait,' he said. 'And the hospital will phone you.'

'But it's two days,' insisted Trevor. 'She is diabetic. Her heart is bad.' He stopped and licked his lips. 'But you're right, I am being a nuisance. If I'm going to phone more hospitals, I can do that at home.'

'Yes, you can do it better there,' agreed Feliks. 'Your own place, your family round you. No one like me to distract you. Far better.'

Trevor rose. He put on his jacket.

'Thank you for your help and time,' he said fumbling with the buttons. 'Let me give you some money for the calls...' He went for his wallet.

'Forget it,' said Feliks, knowing his wasted time far outweighed the cost of the calls.

'Thank you, thank you,' he said, the wallet still in his hand. 'I shall go home and phone from there.' He took out a card from his wallet and handed it to Feliks. 'Please call me at once if she comes back. Don't worry what time it is.'

'I will,' said Feliks, putting the card on the table and going to the flat door and opening it.

There were the last gestures of thanks and farewell as Feliks saw Trevor to the front door, glad to be rid of the obligation. That's what happens when you offer to help. Next time, shut up. He went into his kitchen and sorted out some sausage, tomato and onion with rye bread for lunch. A quick bite then back to work.

Outside on the street, Trevor hesitated. If he went back to Southend and his mother was in a London hospital then he'd only have to come back again. Was there anywhere nearby he could go on the internet? A café maybe or a library. There used to be a library in Forest Gate, he recalled, on Woodgrange Road. But of course he didn't have a library card.

'You OK?' called Jack.

He was in the front yard, mixing sand and cement in a bucket to make up mortar. And had been about to go out to the garden patio for the water, when he'd spotted Trevor dithering.

'Did you have any luck?' he added.

Trevor peered at him, not recognising him at first. He'd left his glasses at home. Then it clicked, the builder who'd broken the window to get into the flat.

'No luck,' he said. 'She's not in any of the local hospitals. I was thinking of going back to Southend or maybe to an internet café... I don't know what's for the best.'

'Have you reported it to the police?' said Jack.

'Should I?'

He's like a kid, thought Jack. No good in an emergency. But then he could talk, everyone's babysitter.

'Yes,' said Jack. 'If anyone is brought into a hospital and not identified, the hospital will contact the police...' He wasn't sure of this, but it seemed reasonable. 'Do you know Forest Gate police station?'

'Yes,' said Trevor. 'I think so. Is it the one on Romford Road, top of Green Street?'

'That's it.' He thought of offering him a lift, but really it was only ten minutes' walk.

Trevor nodded fervently. 'Yes, yes. I should go there. Report her missing. Maybe they'll know something already. But if not, they won't start looking until she's reported. I must go there right away. I've been so worried, I can't think straight.' He took out a card and gave it to Jack. 'If you hear anything please phone me.'

'Of course I will.' He put the card in his overalls pocket, considered for a second, then added, 'I'll run you to the police station.'

Chapter 7

Jack fixed the back window straight after his lunch. Well, a temporary job. He'd screwed a bit of board over it. He wasn't going to do more than that. Let Feliks do it himself. Even a small window can take a couple of hours to do properly, what with buying the glass and putty.

Before getting back to pointing, Jack had attached his block and tackle at the top of his tower. He'd only used it once before and was beginning to think it a needless expense. But with this sort of job, it would save a lot of sweat humping all those buckets of mortar up to the top. And a lot safer too as the alternative was to climb up encumbered with buckets.

A neat little machine, it was, with three pulleys. A site engineer had tried to explain to Jack how it worked and he half understood. The bucket weighed effectively a third of its weight when attached to the block and tackle, but you had three times as much rope to pull up. So he had to pull on 24 metres of rope to get the bucket up 8 metres. Something like that. Anyway, a lot easier than carrying buckets up, and he'd have a lot to get up before the job was done.

Of course, it had taken him twenty minutes untangling the rope. The last time he'd used the block and tackle, he was in a rush to get away. And he'd just thrown the gear in the bag, as he had a date with that blonde woman, what was her name? He'd taken her up the hill in Chingford with his telescope as she'd said she wanted to come. It wasn't as if he'd forced her. Yes, it was a muddy walk up, but fancy wearing those heels. She was exhausted by the climb, and hardly interested in the view through the telescope and what he had to say about the moon and its craters. A disaster of a date. He cringed as he recalled her sullen over the pizza they had afterwards in Pizza Express, going on and on about the mud on her shoes and tights.

Gloria, that was her name.

End of this job, he'd make sure the rope was coiled tidily, ready for use next time. Such a pain taking out a tangle. Then another interruption, seeing Trevor to the police station. He might've gone in with him too, the man seemed so helpless, but parking around there was a chore. He'd stayed a minute or so making sure Trevor didn't back out. He didn't seem to want to go in, hesitating at the door. Jack could sympathise there; cop shops are never comfortable places. But in the end, Trevor went in. And Jack left him.

No wonder Jack never made any money. Giving lifts, fixing windows, all for nothing. But he'd accepted long ago he was never going to get rich. He hadn't the drive, wasn't ruthless enough to be a millionaire.

Water was needed to make up the mortar, and an extra bucket of it to keep the bricks wet while he worked. A visit to the loo too, all that coffee was going through him. He took the two buckets to the patio and left them by the outside tap. Jack went to the French windows which were wide open. Carefully, he peered inside. Jean was on the sofa with Lily on her lap. She was reading her a story from a large picture book.

Jack tapped on the window. When she looked up, he said:

'Can I use the loo?'

'Of course. Would you like a coffee?'

'That would be nice. Where is the toilet?'

'Under the stairs or there's one in the bathroom up top.'

Jack headed off.

When he returned, two coffees were on the low table, Lily was on the carpet doing a large-piece jigsaw, and Jean was clearly waiting for him. He did like her; she was attractive and easy to talk to, but this was a complicated set up. But then Mike had his eye fixed elsewhere. Surely the marriage was kaput?

She said, 'A quick coffee then I must be off to see my solicitor.'

'For the divorce?' he said cautiously.

'Yes.' She sighed. 'I've put it off for too long. All the signs have been there for an age. Never believe anyone who says a baby brings couples back together. A romantic myth, in this marriage anyway. But at least he was working at the theatre when Lily was born, and could take over during the day when I could catch up on sleep or write.' She threw up her hands. 'What's the point going over old ground?' She half laughed. 'He was the bread winner for a while. Not the last 18 months. A convenience, I suppose. He annoys me with his slobby habits, but I've put up with it, so I could get on with my work. It wasn't as if I had a lover. So we had a routine, or so I thought. It never occurred to me until the last few days that he was having it off with the cleaner. I should've guessed earlier. I don't know how long it's been going on. The first time! How dare he tell me that.' She stopped as if aware she was saying too much.

'Maybe if you hadn't found out...' said Jack, unsure of the direction of his thought.

'I could go on living the lie...' She flapped a hand dismissively. 'He makes a bit of money dealing. I don't know how much he makes, hardly enough to fuel his own habit. And how's that going to end? They'll catch him one day. Then what? I turned a blind eye, I shouldn't have, not bringing up a child together. But all this time, with her! What a snake in the grass, what a rat!'

'Which animal do you prefer?' he said.

She half laughed, considering the possibilities. 'A cockroach,' she said at last, 'then I could put my foot on it. Crunch and crackle.'

'That's a lot of hate.'

'It's what betrayal does,' she said, then didn't speak for a while. 'How about you and your ex?' she said at last.

'Well, I don't hate her,' he said. 'I did, but not for long. I deserved it when she threw me out. I was a drunk, a useless sot. Useless to her, to my daughter, and to the world...' He shuddered as the time came back to him. 'That was a bad time. Sleeping rough, drinking rotgut, a pathetic lump. I hadn't a cell of self control. I'd lost any sense of purpose.'

'I'm surprised you can talk about it,' she said.

'You have to talk about it, says Alcohol Halt. That's my group. Admit it to the world, and to yourself.'

He stopped; she was holding his hand. He would have pulled her to him, but she indicated the child with a ring of dolls round the jigsaw.

'You would be good for me,' she said, hushed.

She squeezed his hand, he squeezed back, pressing his knee against hers. They looked into each other's eyes, catching the rhythm of their breathing. She pressed a finger against her own lips and kissed it, then pressed it against his. She held it there, massaging his lips; he closed his eyes, enclosed in the pressure of her finger, knee against knee, hands clasped. Time disappeared in the three points of contact.

And then there were four. The clammy hands of a child pulling at him and her mother until she had seated herself in Jean's lap, the queen enthroned.

Jack separated from Jean. He drank coffee without looking at her, shivering. There was no doubt what would have happened but for the child.

Perhaps as well.

He looked up. She was looking at him.

'I must go to Stratford,' she half whispered.

He nodded. 'I've work to do.'

Neither moved. But they were detaching, like two snails having met on a garden path.

She rose, holding Lily. 'Take your coffee out with you, Jack. I need to shut the French windows.'

Jack stood up with his cup.

She said, 'How will you go to the loo if I lock up?'

'I've peed in a bucket before.'

'No, no. I'll give you the spare key.' And then added, 'Is your offer still on for tonight?'

'It was never retracted.'

'I'll be there.'

Chapter 8

'The cow got me sacked.'

Mandy and Mike were in bed. They'd smoked rock and then made love, getting more savage as the effects wore off. And then he was done, and she was nowhere. Deflated, without more drugs to lift her. What's the point of one blow, she thought. A brief high and then such a downer. You have to follow it up, or you are in the pits.

He was alright. Look at the pig, asleep, contented. He'd just used her, then threw her away like a sugary bag when he'd had his doughnut.

She was angry, she was restless, she was unhappy. The glass jar lay on the bedside chair, pierced foil over its orifice, black sludge at the bottom. Was it worth another burn? She picked it up by the neck, and flicked the lighter into flame. Then began heating the bottom of the jar, keeping the flame moving, so as not to crack the jar. She did this for a minute or two, until the jar became too hot to hold. Squealing, she put it down.

Useless, no fumes were coming off. The stuff was burnt out. Like she was.

She rolled on to her back. The world had come back with a vengeance. She covered her eyes with her arm and wept silently. It was all so hopeless: no job, no money, and no rock. Why had he come over with such a tiddly piece?

Because he'd sold it to that whore, Saffron. For a poke, no doubt.

She turned on her side, and watched him, his head on the pillow, eyes closed. He was a handsome, smug toad. Didn't deserve to keep that body with all his weed smoking, but then she could talk. She rarely said no to a spliff or his rock. And she was getting tubby around the midriff. Mike said it was cosy, but she'd need to get it off if she was still to play younger parts. If she was to play any parts, the way the acting world was going. But she'd need to cut out the munchies post blast, to have any hope. The pizzas and Indian takeaways. They'd have to go. A clear out of body and soul.

The cow had sacked her.

She could stab him, lying there so vulnerable, so few hairs on his chest. Scratch his eyes out for that petty bit of rock and that useless screw. He'd come in, and all he wanted to do was talk about his own troubles. They were nothing compared to her own.

Mike rubbed his eyes and opened them, blinking in the light.

'She's off to a solicitor this afternoon to start divorce proceedings,' he said drowsily.

She leaned over him, her breasts lightly brushing his chest, and massaged his eyebrows.

He lifted her off. 'No more, Mandy. Twice in a day is all I can manage. I'm out of puff.'

She pouted at the rejection, hating him, needing him, while for him, she suspected, she was just an additional spliff. A top up. She had to say no, more often. And mean it. Hold him off, make him want her. Oh, but he could too easily turn her round.

'She's upset everything,' he said. 'So busy these days, we just meet for a moment in the kitchen, or to pass Lily on... But with you and her busyness, it sort of worked. Me and you fitting in to her schedule.'

'Till this morning,' she added, needlessly.

She laid back on the pillow. Sex wasn't on, maybe she could stir him or maybe just be snarled at. She wanted to weep on his chest, but he didn't like her doing that. Last time, he'd told her he wasn't her sponge; she shouldn't drag him into her misery.

'I went to the Job Centre earlier,' she said. 'I hate that hole. Thought police. They turn you inside out for a few quid. What was I to say when the woman asked me why I left my job? It's no good lying, they only have to make a phone call to check. I had to say she sacked me. And then the woman kept asking me for the reason.' She gave a mirthless laugh. 'I wasn't going to tell her the client caught me in bed with her husband. And the agency kicked me out.'

Mike laughed. She dug him in the stomach. Not that hard, but hard enough to make her point.

'It wasn't funny, Mike. The woman was writing it all on her computer, busy busy. I said I was sloppy at the job. What else could I say? Oh, did she lecture me!'

'They train them by getting them to tear the legs off spiders.'

Mandy blew a raspberry. 'The bitch said I'd be sanctioned for three months.'

'What does that mean?'

'No damned money.'

'What a bummer!'

'I'm stuffed,' she exclaimed. 'I can't get a regular job. They always ask for a reference from your last employer. And if they contact the agency, I get stuck with gross misconduct.'

'What are you going to do?'

She sighed. 'The cow, the hifalutin, toffee nosed cow. Your missus. The way she pulled my hair and walloped me round the face. I could scratch her eyes out.'

'What are you going to do?' he said again.

'If I could get some acting work... They're only interested in your last acting work. So I won't have to mention the sacking. But if that doesn't come off,' she flapped her hands weakly in the air, 'then I'll lose this place. No money to pay the rent. I'll be out.' She stopped, then added wistfully, 'I wish you'd brought my shoe back. Twenty five quid that pair cost. Almost new. I've one other pair and they're pretty worn out.'

'Sorry. Next time.'

'You couldn't loan me some cash, Mike?' She had a hand on his thigh, the fingers slipping upwards.

He unpeeled the hand, and said, 'I've an idea for you. Make you some money.'

'How?'

'Fancy a bit of dealing?'

She was silent a while. The conversation had come up before when she was desperate. But she'd never fancied the risk or the dodgy characters. Or had the capital to get started.

'You could limit yourself to chicks.'

'If I lose this place,' she said bitterly, 'I'm done for.' Could she deal? There was of course the option of audition queues. But that was so dispiriting, with all those kids fresh out of drama school. She knew well enough she was virtually at the end of that road. And needed another road, quick. One that didn't need a reference from her last employer.

'How do I get a stake?' she said. 'I'm broke. Unless you...'

He kissed her briefly. She tried pulling him to her, but he was away.

'Jean owes you,' he said. 'She sacked you. It's only fair. Call it redundancy.' He didn't speak for a couple of seconds, then added, 'You still got the key to the house?'

'I lost my knickers, one shoe and a sock,' she said with a short laugh. 'But I kept the key.'

'So listen. You need a few hundred. Get it. Then I buy for both of us, from my dealer. And you find your customers. I'll leave that to you, just don't hustle mine.'

She was listening, bursting for a puff. Another reason for dealing, to keep herself going and not wait on lover boy.

'She's off out tomorrow afternoon,' he went on. 'It's a

regular thing, with one of her writing mates. They help each other with Skype tutorials, that sort of blarney. Now, if I was to take Lily to my mother's in Romford...' He stopped and waited for her.

'The house will be empty,' she said thoughtfully.

'Anyone could break in. And Jean could so easily lose a fair bit of gear.'

'Her stuff,' she said, her tongue lolling in her cheek.

'A few bits of mine to make it look real. But a burglar wouldn't be interested in my guitars.'

Chapter 9

'This place stinks like a whorehouse,' exclaimed Feliks, waving his arms like a floppy puppet.

'Doesn't bother you when you want a trick,' retorted Saffron.

They were in her sitting room, on the sofa with its fluffy cushions. The room was thick with smoke and cheap perfume.

'I don't like it when you smoke in here,' he said, sitting down. 'You could burn the house down.'

'It's crack. It's safe,' she said with a shrug. 'Just heat from a lighter.'

'It's such a waste of your money.'

'I earn it. I spend it.' She turned to him. 'You get your rent. So what's the problem?'

'I don't like to see all that money burning.'

'That's my business. Anyway, I need my burn. This job isn't easy, you know. I have to keep up the chat. Treat everyone like he's the first I've had in a year.'

'You should get an Oscar, my dear. But I didn't come to talk about your acting skills.'

She looked at the wall clock. A regular was coming in twenty minutes and she wanted some blow beforehand. She wasn't giving Feliks another freebie, even if there was time. Business was business, as he was quick to point out.

'So what is it?' she said warily.

He gave her a bright smile, then said, 'I'm here about the rent.'

'I paid you,' she said, with some annoyance.

'I'm putting it up to three fifty.' The smile had switched off.

She threw up her arms. 'You money grabbing freak....' Then stopped herself, a string of insults on the tip of her tongue. She needed the flat. She'd been evicted a few times; landlords didn't like business girls. 'That's one hell of a leap, Feliks.'

'This is a working premises,' he said reasonably. 'Not simply a place to live, and I have to take that into account. It's not everyone would have you, Saffron. And I give you protection.'

'I pay you for that.'

'Sure, but having me on site, that's got to be worth more. So three fifty – and you can smoke less from now on.'

She considered her options as she watched him scrape cement from under his fingernails with her nail file. This was only the start, she knew. Feliks could keep coming round, making up a figure. But moving out was such a hassle, and yes, he was here when she had a troublesome punter, even if that cost her fifty a call. She could, though, offer a barter.

'Keep it at three hundred and I'll give you two tricks a week.'

He laughed. 'Always a player, Saffron. Except with the smoking. Cut it out and build up a nest egg. Join me in the property game.'

She ignored the advice. 'So what about my offer?'

He shrugged and gave a sly smile. 'Who said I need them?'

'Why, you got someone else on the go?'

He rubbed his thumb and forefingers in a secret gesture. 'If it goes right. Internet dating. They're so desperate. You only have to tell them you want a family, flatter them...'

'You're such a charmer, Feliks.'

She wanted him to leave, so she could have a blow before the next punter arrived. But she couldn't just show him the door. Not mid-negotiations.

'Women are so obsessed with their bodies...' he said as if telling her a deep secret. 'So tell them how beautiful they are, what a wonderful dress, what lovely hands...' He paused, considering. 'If I can accumulate them?'

'What?' she said, puzzled.

'The tricks. Two a week, you said. But what if I don't use them? I want to carry them over.'

'Like holidays.' She laughed at the old rake. 'Sure, carry them over. Why – you could hold off for a month or so, then have two every day for a week.' She could see from his smirk, he liked the idea. 'So we've a deal then?'

He held out his hand. She shook it.

'I'll take one on account. Now,' he said. 'To seal it.'

She cursed inwardly. There wouldn't be time for a blow if she agreed. But she couldn't get out of it, unless she wanted a row. Besides, he might smack her one. It paid to keep him cool. Oh, but she needed that blow! At least Feliks didn't hang about, such a busy man. If she could do him quickly, a blow might just be possible.

'Come on,' she said and led the way to the bedroom.

Chapter 10

Jack washed his bucket and trowels under the yard tap. Quite a good day's work, in spite of the interruptions. The sun had escaped from a cloud, brightening the gardens and rooftops. It was warm on his neck and face. There was a slight breeze in the treetops. Leaf fall had hardly begun and there were flowers here and there in the garden.

The cement mixer next door was chugging away. Did the man ever stop?

His own work up top had become automatic. His mind drifted, as he pushed mortar between the rows of bricks. Half a bucket was all he made up at a time as the mortar became useless once it began setting. He kept the bricks wet from another bucket containing water, slapping it on liberally with a wide paint brush. Every so often, he came down to ground level to make up mortar and bring up water. He'd attach a bucket to the hook of the block and tackle, climb to the top and haul it up. The simple machine pleased him, the way the rope ran through the pulleys. Making the work easier and safer.

But his major preoccupation was the lady of the house. The work barely needed thought, and his mind settled again and again on the coffee break in the sitting room. What would have happened if the infant hadn't been there?

Part of him thought just as well Lily was there. Jean was still living with her husband; the relationship was complicated enough without him being part of it. But the animal in him thought, what the hell! Take what's on offer. The same track playing over and over while he pointed the brickwork, climbing up and down the scaffolding tower.

She was attractive, she was a good listener, she wanted it.

If Mike had had Lily this afternoon... They would have made love, surely enough. And if her husband had come back, burst into the bedroom, like a replay of the morning with the parts shifted, how would Mike have reacted? Consumed with jealousy? Or saying – all yours, mate, I'm off to my dealer...

At least Jean was the client. Mike might, in that circumstance, rant and rage, throw a jealous strop, but couldn't sack him. Though his presence, if they went any further, would sour the atmosphere.

Just as well nothing had happened.

He dropped the tools in the bucket. Time to go. He pondered about his block and tackle. Would it be safe up there on the tower? The garden gate would be locked all night. It would be a hassle to steal with its thirty metres of rope. And he'd screwed it on tight. The thief would need a wrench to get it off. And it would be such a chore to take down every night.

It'd be all right, he persuaded himself.

Before leaving the patio with his washed buckets and tools, he looked in through the French windows. They were locked, the way Jean had left them earlier, the room empty. He'd hoped she'd be back by now. A glimpse, a word or two, a touch. Reassurance that she was coming tonight. But if she had returned, she wasn't in the sitting room. And he didn't want to rap on the glass, in case Mike was back.

And what would he say to him?

Jack went down the side path and out the garden door. He couldn't see her car parked by the roadside. She had a silver Audi, he'd noted. He couldn't see it, which didn't mean it wasn't there, as he himself had had to park his van a hundred yards away. She could be on either side, up or down, or most likely not here at all.

Her face lit with passion, her chestnut hair and blue eyes, beautiful even in anger. Her finger on his lips. In those

63

moments, he'd wanted to pull her to him. But the infant, the passion killer...

And Mia would be with them tonight. Well, it would be civilised then. If Mia liked her. Always a consideration.

Was Jean thinking of him now? She was attracted, but to more than sex? That was the unanswerable, which hadn't stopped him coming up with a variety of answers through the afternoon. She had her work, and praise heaped on her as well as cash. Did she need a builder who just scraped by?

She did, she didn't. Alternative universes had formed and dissolved, as he'd trowelled mortar into the brickwork.

Jack locked his tools in the van, took a last look up and down the street – and drove off.

He was only five minutes from home. And once there, had to park. His road was full of cars both sides. It would've been easier to have left the vehicle where he was working and walked home. He drove up and down the road. It was so stupid, this, with every space filled, many who didn't even live here. How much time the world wasted, driving up and down, to find a parking spot.

There wasn't one, not within 150 metres. And he gave up, driving back to Clova Road. Hoping the parking space he'd left was still there. But it wasn't. Filled by a silver Audi.

She was home. And so what? He wasn't about to knock on her door and suggest they go upstairs. He wanted to be away and out of this space, his head free of this fruitless longing. Ahead of him a car pulled out. Quickly, Jack drew up, and as soon as the space was free, claimed it. He was almost opposite the house. But could see no one through the curtains. Likely she was in the kitchen, making some food for her and Lily.

Jack locked his van, and was walking away, when, from across the street, the black woman from next door hailed him. She rushed over, her face drawn and tense, bosom bursting out of her red dress.

'Have you seen Mike?' she demanded.

'He's been out all afternoon,' he said.

'Yes, but is he back?' she pleaded, as if somehow Jack could produce him from his pocket.

'Not as far as I know,' said Jack, unable to magic him there.

She was clenching and unclenching her fists. 'I so need a blow. Where is the bastard when you need him?'

She had lost interest in Jack, looking up and down the road, obviously on the look out for her supplier.

He set off to walk home. Saffron was going up and down the road, as if unsure which way Mike might be coming. Jack wondered if Jean really knew the extent of his dealing. All the nasty people involved, and stoned customers ever ready to welsh on their dealer. Such a dirty business.

A little way up the road, Jack crossed over and turned down a side road. There was Mike, on the other side of the street, coming his way. Mike hailed him and crossed over.

'How's it going?' said Mike.

His hair was roughed up, T-shirt half in and half out of his jeans, suggesting to Jack he'd been at the cleaner's place. Unless he had someone else on the go.

'A good start,' said Jack, knowing it was simply an opening. Mike cared little about how the pointing was progressing.

'Is she back?' Mike asked.

'Your missus?' said Jack.

Mike nodded.

'She just got back,' he said.

'Did she say where she'd been?'

'I haven't talked to her since she's got back,' said Jack. 'But when she left, she said she was going to see her solicitor.'

Mike smiled ruefully. His teeth were sound, but going a little brown. 'You know what that's about? Don't you?'

Jack nodded. 'I picked it up from this morning's racket. And she told me.'

Mike nudged him. 'Fancy her, do you?'

What was he to say? 'She's not my sort...' he stammered.

Mike rolled his lips. 'Just as well. She talks the talk but she's as frigid as the Greenland ice cap.' He laughed. 'Unless you fancy a challenge?'

Distilled hatred. Pointless asking Mike for details.

'It's obvious you're not getting on,' said Jack, for something neutral to say.

'You can have her, mate, with my blessing.'

Said with such venom that Jack knew it was a useless offer.

'That black woman next door is on the look out for you,' he said.

'Saffron,' said Mike between gritted teeth. 'What state was she in?'

'Pretty shaky.'

'Better get there then,' he exclaimed. 'Can't have her going elsewhere.'

He gave a wave, turned about and was striding down the road, every so often breaking into a run. A man on a mission.

Jack strolled home.

Chapter 11

When Jack arrived at his flat, Mia was there. She was slumped out on the sofa, half reading a teen mag. She was in her school uniform, a sky blue shirt and navy blue trousers, her long hair tied back in a ponytail. A full school bag was dumped on the floor.

She looked up from her reading, 'You could've washed up, Dad. I can't get to the sink to fill a kettle.'

How like her mother she sounded.

'Sorry,' he said. 'Had to rush out this morning.'

'I think you should do it right away.'

He glared at her. He wasn't going to be bullied by his daughter. Or get into a fight.

'Let me sit down for a minute.' He took the armchair and laid back, quelling himself. 'How was your day?' An easy question while he calmed down.

'My class teacher hates me,' she said screwing up her face. She slapped down her magazine. 'Mum shouldn't have told her off.'

'What for?'

'For accepting slipshod work,' she said wearily, 'or so Mum says it was.'

'That's what happens when your mum's a school head.' His sympathies were with the teacher. Alison could certainly give a tongue lashing as he knew from experience. 'What do you know about her date tonight?'

She shrugged. 'Some computer thing. Seems a bit of a plonker to me.'

Jack laughed. Mia rarely approved of her parents' love lives.

'He's so old,' she insisted. 'Nearly fifty. It's crazy really. She tells me off for my English. His is worse, a lot worse.

And all moony and drippy.' She chuckled, 'I caught her Skypeing. I couldn't believe the soppy stuff they were saying to each other.'

'Like what?'

Mia said in an attempt at a foreign accent, 'Your eyes are like midnight pools.'

Jack shifted uncomfortably. He'd been as bad this afternoon. 'Where's he from?'

'Can't remember. Got a weird name. I think he's rich. A property developer.'

'You must be joking. Your mother and a property developer!'

'She said she's fed up with penniless liars.'

'So she's trying rich liars instead.'

'Exactly what I said.'

'None of my business, as I am sure she'd tell me,' said Jack with a shrug. He rose. 'I'd better wash up and put the kettle on. You do your homework.'

'Hardly got any.'

'Do it anyway. We're off out later.'

'Where to?'

'Wanstead Flats. You forgotten?'

She clicked her fingers. 'The conjunction of Venus and Jupiter. I told my science teacher. She wants a photo. Better charge the camera batteries.'

Jack said carefully, 'Someone's joining us.'

'Who?'

'A woman from where I'm working.'

'So I'm playing gooseberry. Great.' She pouted, folding her arms.

'Of course not. I thought you'd like to meet her. She's a writer.'

'What's she written?'

'Suspense fantasy, I think she said. She said she'd send an ebook. Might have come already.'

'I'll see if it's here.'

Jack's laptop was on the table. She turned it on.

'Just check if it's come. Then homework,' he said.

'Nag, nag,' she said rolling her eyes. 'You're both as bad as one another.'

Suits me, thought Jack as he left for the kitchen. Equality was better than being worse.

The sink bowl was exactly as he'd left it in the morning. Not that he'd expected the washing up fairy. It just hadn't looked so bad in the morning. Max had offered to do it last night, but Jack refused to let him. Mentoring didn't include the dishes, he'd said adamantly. He'd do it when Max had gone, he'd told him. But he hadn't. And this morning, he'd added to it.

He turned away from his negligence. What food did they have? In the fridge, he found two eggs, some cheese, and half an onion. An omelette then. In the cupboard was a tin of beans (how had that escaped him this morning?) and a few slices of bread. That'd do. They could pop in the Co-op on the way back home, get some supper, stuff for breakfast, and for both their lunches tomorrow.

When he turned back, the stack of dirty dishes asserted their challenge. One he had to beat, as that was all the crockery he had. Now he recalled why he hadn't done it this morning – no washing up liquid. He searched under the sink for a substitute. Could you use window wash? He never used it for windows anyway. Surely it would be OK if you rinsed it off. Wasn't it all the same stuff in different bottles?

He read the label. The ingredients meant little, but there was an instruction: *not to be used on items for food*. What on earth did they put in the stuff?

Not that one licked windows.

Jack piled all the clean dishes and pots on the kitchen table and filled the empty bowl with warm water and a couple of squirts of window wash. He was surprised how much foam it produced. It could double as bubblebath. He washed the items, putting them back on the table, away from the dirty stuff. When he'd washed them all, he looked at the foamy pile on the table. Assume they are covered in a deadly poison, he thought. He filled the bowl with clean water and had the cold tap running. Each item was swilled in the bowl of water and then rinsed under the tap before being put on the drying rack.

He wiped the table and hid the window cleaner in the sink cupboard. No one would know what he'd used. But he must buy some washing up liquid. He put the kettle on; that was the point of all this. A cup of tea. Then something to eat.

When he came back into the sitting room, Mia was reading from his laptop. She looked up guiltily. Moving a few papers, he put her tea down on the coffee table, and glanced at the screen. Definitely not school work.

'She's good,' exclaimed Mia.

'Have you got to the sex yet?'

'No,' said Mia. 'How do you know?'

'She thought it might be a bit raunchy for you.'

Mia grinned. 'I'll tell you if it's unsuitable.'

'Homework,' insisted Jack.

'I'll just finish this chapter.'

Chapter 12

Jean and Lily were in the kitchen, seated at the table. She was half talking to her daughter, half thinking of the builder. He'd gone by the time she'd got back. She realised at once, as she'd taken his parking place. She'd rushed back from the solicitor in the hope of catching him. Quite teenage really, taken over by a few gestures and words; someone looking in your eyes.

She must sort out her life. Get rid of Mike. *The* priority. She'd known that for ages. Simply got used to him being around. But after his shenanigans this morning... No, no, clear him out. Then take on an au pair or a nanny. An au pair would be cheaper, but she wouldn't be full time with Lily, whereas a nanny could take charge much of the time. She'd have to do her sums; there were expenses coming up.

Jack was sensitive, for a builder. Though really, what did she know about builders? Must they all be brutish hod carriers? She had too many prejudices.

She put the dirty dishes in the dishwasher.

'Did you enjoy the fish fingers?' she said to Lily.

Lily nodded.

'When are you going to talk, dearest?' She half laughed. 'When there's someone intelligent to talk to. I shall have to read improving books.'

The front door slammed. She almost leapt from her skin. He was back. She certainly wouldn't ask him where he'd been. But it shouldn't be a threat whenever the door slammed. There were only three of them in the house. It should be easy enough to get on. Except when one of them sleeps with the cleaner... Of course, she might have had the builder this afternoon. But then Mike had started it, granting her carte blanche.

He came into the kitchen, sweaty, eyes narrowed. He's stoned, she thought. Again. She sat down not sure what to say. Mike went straight to the breadbin as if she and Lily weren't present.

She said, 'I went to the solicitor.'

'And?' Having got his bread, he was searching the fridge.

'It should be straightforward,' she said. 'A couple of months.'

'Can't be soon enough,' he said, taking items out and putting them on the side.

Neither spoke for a while. He began buttering the mixed-grain slices. She wanted to say something about the mess he was making, but thought what's the point? He hadn't even washed his hands and his fingers were all over the cheese.

'I want half the house,' he said.

'I don't think so,' she said.

He turned on her waving a knife. 'Give me a good reason why not, seeing I put my money into it..'

'I'll be granted custody of Lily,' she said, 'and for that the court will say I should have the house.'

'What do I get?'

'What do you deserve, Mike?'

'We bought this place together...'

'You haven't paid any of the mortgage since you lost your job.'

'What about the furniture?' he exclaimed. 'We bought that together, the carpets. I did some of the decorating...'

'You want to pull the wallpaper off the walls?' she exclaimed. 'We'll see what the court says about furniture.'

'You've got this all worked out, you and your lesbian solicitor.' He slapped the knife on the table. 'You're going to clean me out.'

'I've Lily to consider,' she said, trying to keep her tone reasonable. 'We need a home. We need furniture. And there will be childminding to pay for, one way or another.'

'Where do you expect me to live?'

'You can shack up with your cleaner.'

'You got her sacked!'

He shook his hands in fury. Grabbed a sandwich and threw it at her, following it up with the cheese. A bottle of pickle smashed against the wall, splattering pickle and glass over Jean.

Lily was crying, clutching a leg of the table. Jean brought her out from under the table, kneeling down to her height.

'There, there, luvey. Don't cry.'

Mike was leaning against the sink, hands clutching the edge, face white.

'I put my hard-earned cash into this house,' he seethed, 'bought my share of furniture, I decorated...and I walk away with nothing. You and that hoity-toity solicitor are going to carve me to the bone.'

She was breathing heavily, wiping herself off with kitchen roll, watching him for sudden movement, holding Lily with her other arm. There was glass and pickle scattered about her. It was dangerous and smelly.

'Ms High and Mighty,' he continued. 'The great writer, the boon to mankind. Coining it in.' He thumped his chest. 'Me? I've had some bad luck. Do I get sympathy? No, just a kick when I'm down.' He imitated her in a silly voice, 'When you going to get a job? When you gonna stop smoking weed?' He threw up his hands. 'Is it any wonder I go elsewhere for comfort? That'd be a fine thing round here.'

'You've got talent, Mike,' Jean said cautiously. 'But you kill it when you smoke weed all day. I haven't heard you playing your guitar or keyboard in months. Why should I keep you?'

'It's all judgement with you. Watching, ticking off. You'd think I was eating babies.' He picked up his plate with its remaining food, and strode across the kitchen. At the door, he turned. 'I have rights too. You're going to regret taking me on. You sanctimonious bitch.'

He slammed the door after him.

She waited, to make sure he wasn't coming back, letting the vibrations die. She was spent, exhausted by the row, his sudden violence. If that bottle had hit her or Lily... How could she work here with him around? She'd always be listening for him. Mental note, no criticism. Don't wind him up.

Either he goes or she must. That was plain. A temporary move in her case. Until matters were sorted out by the court. She'd intended to ask him to look after Lily this evening, for a few hours. There was no point asking now; he'd delight in saying no. If he bothered to answer her. Tomorrow, she'd look for a childminder, somewhere she could take Lily while she worked.

Where? How? So much to do. She had an online course she was due to be running in a couple of days. Would she have to cancel it? Send them back their cash.

If she couldn't work here, then she'd have to find somewhere else. A hotel? Had it really got to that? Think of the expense... But what were her choices?

She sat Lily in a chair, wiped her face and gave her some orange slices. Tried to be as calming as she could, as she cleared up the cheese and bread, the bits of glass and pickle.

Chapter 13

Mia and Jack left the house to walk to Wanstead Flats. The sun was egg yellow, low in the western sky. Too low for shadows. Geese flew over in a squawky V, perhaps heading for the flats too. The air was still, with more day in it than night.

Mia had her camera round her neck. Jack had a tripod over his shoulder. In his backpack was a thermos of tea and a pair of binoculars. They wore woolly hats and light jackets. They wouldn't be out long, an hour at the most.

Cars filled both sides of Earlham Grove. The plane trees were fully canopied, the leaves larger than hands, deep green in their last days before the mother tree cut off sustenance. Two women in burqas came past, one with a pushchair. Jack purposely looked away, finding their covered faces difficult in spite of its commonness. Though he could understand the purpose of their veil. They refused to be part of his fantasies, to engage with his maleness in any way. Maybe that was his difficulty.

A black man approached, most definitely eyeing Mia. Should he, her father, shroud her? Or perhaps put the man's eyes out. And his own too, as he caught a woman on the other side of the road. Thank God his thoughts were secret. Keep busy, don't let sex take you over. Don't tell.

He turned, checking the sky where the sun was about to set. It was clear of cloud. Important, as that was where the conjunction would be seen. Of course, the planets were there already but the bright light of the sun hid them. Once the sun had set, then Venus and Jupiter would appear, but only for about half an hour, before they in turn set.

'She writes really well,' said Mia.

For a second he didn't know what she was talking about, then realised it was Jean's book.

'Did you do your homework?' he said.

She was silent, before saying, 'I'll do it when we get back.'

He didn't say anything. It had been thoughtless of him to tell her about the book in the first place. He could've anticipated this happening. Now she was telling him the plot. And he was at once confused: the odd names of the people and places, the comings and goings. He let her ramble, hoping she wouldn't ask him any questions.

A man was cycling up the pavement towards them. The road is clear, thought Jack, hardly a car on it, why take the pavement? The man had no right to be here. Mia went to the side, Jack continued down the middle and the man swerved past him. There were too many things to annoy you in the city. Cars parking everywhere, bikes on pavements, dog shit, litter, eyes following you, clothing, non clothing. He should stay inside, draw the curtains and watch the soaps. Except they would annoy him too.

He was stressed just walking down the road, and knew it was because he was meeting Jean. On edge already, anticipating her company. And wondering how he and she would cope with the addition of Mia. They mustn't be lovey-dovey, had to include her. No holding hands or kisses. And Mia herself. Would she and Jean get on? Mia could be sullen, a heavy presence.

They turned the corner on to the high street. Just up the rise, past the shops and the Co-op supermarket, was Forest Gate station where they'd arranged to meet. She wasn't there yet, or at least he couldn't see her.

They stopped at the station. A train had come in, and people were streaming out the entrance, the tail end of the rush hour. He and Mia stood back against the wall of the station, to be out of the human traffic. He watched down the hill for her. That's the way she'd come; she'd said that she would walk up. It was half seven, the time they'd arranged.

Mia was trying out the camera, snapping people and road traffic, playing with the zoom.

Had Jean changed her mind? He looked at his watch; it was only two minutes past the time. The crowd had gone. They were alone by the entrance. He couldn't see her down the hill. This was hardly a date. Not important, easy not to come. He would pretend in the morning that it didn't matter; that he'd hardly expected her.

'What does she look like?' said Mia looking about her.

'About my height, my age, reddish hair, good looking...,' adding, 'well I think she is.'

'You'd make a bad police witness,' she said.

'It's hard describing people,' he said, 'beyond male female, black white, tall short, old young, fat thin.'

'How long do we give her?'

Jack thought, until I know she isn't coming. He didn't have her phone number which would have saved some anguish. Hadn't thought of it, being too in the moment.

'Fifteen minutes,' he said.

'That woman in the car is waving at us,' said Mia, indicating a car that had stopped at the roadside.

Jack looked to where Mia was pointing. It was her. He hadn't expected her in a vehicle. She couldn't park there by the traffic lights. He waved her to drive up ahead. She nodded and she went on with the green light. They followed, across Forest Lane, past the small shops on the narrow pavement, watching her, waiting for her to halt, Jack wondering how she'd be. She'd pulled in just before the bus stop at the medical centre.

'Get in,' she said when they arrived.

Mia at once climbed in the front, leaving Jack a little resentful as he took a seat in the back with Lily in the child-seat. He lay the tripod in the well.

'Seat belts on,' said Jean.

Jack and Mia did as she bid.

'Where to?' said Jean, turning to him.

He could barely reply, her face there, speaking to him directly. He wanted to touch her cheek, knowing in the look that the afternoon had been real.

'About half a mile up,' he said. 'There's a parking place on the flats.'

'I know it,' she said, and turned away. He felt a pang of rejection. Of course it wasn't, but it was as if she'd gone from him, nonsensical or not. She pulled out in the traffic. 'I didn't mean to come by car,' she added, glancing at him through the mirror, 'but I had to bring Lily. The situation at home is bad.'

Jack guessed that meant a row.

Mia said, 'I really like your book, Jean. Can I call you Jean?'

'Of course, you can. Mia, isn't it? How far have you got?'

'About six chapters in. It's really exciting.'

'Where have you got to?'

'When Ansty is in the forest, following the fox and she rescues the girl from being tortured...' She added, 'I guessed she would have to meet someone. Have companions. Makes it all the more interesting.'

'It does,' agreed Jean.

Jack felt out of the swing in the back seat. Perhaps he should have read a couple of chapters. But it would only be a few minutes to the parking spot, and he needed the two of them to get on. Or why invite Jean at all? He watched Lily playing with a teddy and a rhinoceros. They were obviously good friends.

'Are you all right back there, Jack?'

'I'm fine,' he said, gratified she was concerned.

'She's a great writer,' exclaimed Mia.

'You've got a fan,' said Jack.

'I'm so glad you like it,' said Jean to Mia.

And Mia was talking about characters and situations,

quite losing Jack. He was in no mood to follow anything more complicated than a nursery rhyme. He gazed out of the window as they passed under the railway bridge of Wanstead Park station. A few cars already had their headlights on, the sun had set but day was refusing to let go.

They'd reached the beginning of the flats on Centre Road, grassy plains on either side. The whole area was about a square mile, flat as the name implied. About a third were football pitches, the rest rough ground, with copses of trees and areas of gorse. The car park they were approaching was popular with model aircraft enthusiasts, precisely because of the car park. They needed hardly venture from their vehicles to fly their pampered models.

Jean pulled in to the cindered area. There were no other cars there. A little of night's gloom was dripping into the eastern sky, the western horizon a blaze of orange red, splintered in thin clouds. Jack and Mia were out of the car quickly, while Jean came round to get Lily out and to lock up.

'Oh,' exclaimed Mia fiddling with the camera. 'My battery is almost out. No, it's totally out. How stupid! I only charged it for an hour before we came out – and it wasn't long enough.'

Jack didn't say anything about the shots she'd been taking at the station. It wouldn't help. To buy batteries would mean driving back to Forest Gate. And really, the camera had been at his place. He could've charged the batteries, if he hadn't been so preoccupied.

'I've a camera you can use,' said Jean. 'I thought it might be useful.' She had a large bag with her, full of things for Lily, and drew out a camera in a case.

'Oh!' exclaimed Mia. 'It's much better than mine. Look, Dad, a DSLR.'

Jean took it out of its case. 'If I put it on automatic for you, Mia. And this twilight setting...' Jack and Mia were round her watching. 'This lever works the zoom. Focus by twisting the lens. And press this to take a photo.' She put the camera round Mia's neck. 'Careful with it. It cost over six hundred quid.'

'Wow. And there's a screw thread for a tripod.'

'Let's get away from the road and the street lights,' said Jack.

He had the tripod over his shoulder, a small rucksack with binoculars and tea on his back. He directed them further into the flats, off the rough, bumpy ground and into an area of football pitches. They walked slowly, at Lily's pace. Mia had Jean's camera proudly round her neck. Every so often, she would stop and take their picture.

Jack thought, this is a family. The happy family of ads and cliché. Never mind that he was divorced and Jean was divorcing; it looked like a family to anyone who might see them walking across the flats together. But there were few to note them: a solitary dog walker, a runner in the distance, and a couple too engaged in the long grass.

Lily was running back and forth between them, Mia in her element snapping away. Jean sidled up to Jack and put an arm round his waist. He slipped his round hers and wondered whether Mia would react to their closeness. But it fell apart when Lily tripped over a grassy hump and needed to be fussed over.

The red glow in the west had become a faint strip along the horizon. Above were a few clouds, charcoal grey, the blue between deepening. The street lights were on along Centre Road. Light pollution was inevitable in London. Their aim was to lessen its effect by going to the middle of the flats. The best that could be done, short of going out to the countryside.

'There's Venus.' Mia pointed out the bright pinprick.

It was in the west, about a third of the way from the zenith; its brightness almost growing by the second.

'Where's Jupiter?' said Jean, turning about and searching the sky.

'Just there, a little way along from Venus,' said Jack. 'You can just see it. There.' He held her arm up and pointed it in the direction. 'See?'

'I've got it,' she said. 'Venus though is a lot brighter.'

'The brightest star in the sky,' said Mia. 'Though it isn't a star, it's a planet, but it's called the evening star and sometimes the morning star. Depending when you see it.'

She had taken the tripod from Jack, and began to set up. Pulling out the three legs to a convenient height, then screwing them tight. Lily was chasing a seagull who knew he could beat her any day of the week, and just hopped away.

Jack and Jean were side by side, holding hands. She kissed a finger and dabbed it on his lips. He held it there and gently bit the tip. Mia was busying herself putting the camera on to the tripod. Lily ran up to her mother, and Jean picked her up.

They watched the two early stars, Venus the brighter and Jupiter like its infant, though it was a hundred times bigger, but so much further from the sun. The gap between them about three moon-widths.

'They're nowhere near each other in reality,' said Jack. 'Hundreds of millions of miles apart.' She nudged her leg next to his as he continued. 'It's our line of sight makes them appear close together.'

'They shouldn't really call it a conjunction,' said Mia taking her first pictures. 'You two are more like a conjunction. Touching.'

Jean moved her leg self-consciously away from Jack.

'More like a conversation,' she went on, 'between friends who don't meet very often.'

Over the next quarter of an hour, Mia would take over a hundred photos, back and forth on the zoom, as the two planets arced to the horizon, to set in their turn, interrupted only by tea and the chocolate fingers that Jean had brought.

PART TWO:
THIS CAN'T GO ON

Chapter 14

The chess game was too vexing for Mike. Too silent, too demanding of his concentration which dwelt on Jean and the intended robbery. From the moment she'd caught them in bed, his finances were on the slide, thumping to zero with the row in the kitchen. Where he'd thrown insults and bottles, and struck nothing.

'Your queen is en prise,' said Feliks.

They were at the table opposite each other, in Feliks' sitting room, the large board between them, the wooden pieces, standard Staunton. Mike had been about to move his black knight, in fact had it in his hand. In a serious game, this would mean he'd have to move the piece and the queen would be gone. But this wasn't serious. Feliks always won, and often pointed out Mike's errors to make some sort of contest of the game.

Mike took a sip of coffee. Feliks only made cheap instant, whereas Jean always bought Italian beans which they ground themselves. This was powdery crap; he'd even told Feliks so, who'd said that at least it was cheap crap. And what could you say to that?

Feliks was going out on one of his assignments, Mike could tell, from the pinkish red shirt he wore, the smart check jacket on the chair. And the smell of his aftershave across the table, certainly not put on for Mike's benefit.

Mike replaced the knight and took up the queen, tentatively moving it above the board.

'Quite a row in your house today,' Feliks smiled, eager for knowledge, man to man.

'There was, wasn't there?' said Mike with a short laugh. At least you could talk to Feliks. He'd be on your side. He understood the way of the world.

'She caught me and Mandy in bed.'

'The cleaner!' chortled Feliks. 'Was she wearing her rubber gloves?'

'She was on top and I was coming, oh was I coming,' exclaimed Mike. 'And Jean flew in like the avenging angel. Dead on cue. She must've been waiting outside the door.'

'Inconsiderate of her,' said Feliks. 'Not to let you finish.'

'She wants a divorce,' said Mike, ignoring his companion's attempt at humour. 'She went to see her solicitor to fill in the papers this afternoon.' He retreated his queen to the back lines, and hesitantly took his hand away. 'Your move.'

'Do you want one?' said Feliks rubbing his chin as he examined the new position.

Mike shrugged. 'It's not the divorce I care about. Our marriage is done for. No sex. Of course, I go elsewhere. What did she think I would do? But the settlement. She's going for the lot.'

'What's the lot?'

Feliks moved his black knight to attack the queen in her fortress.

'I mean everything. The house, the furniture. She gets custody of Lily, and because of that, I lose all but the clothes on my back.'

'Could you go for custody?'

Mike shrugged. 'I could try, except I don't want it. Anyway, the courts always favour the mother. I'd spend a fortune on a lawyer and lose.'

Mike took up his harassed queen. The board was too crowded. His pieces were hemmed in. Feliks was attacking everywhere. He didn't know where to go. Every move was crap.

'Kill her,' said Feliks.

Mike dropped the queen. The pieces scattered as she hit the board. He began replacing them but Feliks' hand went on his.

'Leave them be,' he said. 'You'd have lost in two moves anyway.'

Mike sat back. His neighbour had seen his very core. He had thought of killing Jean, after he'd left her in the kitchen. There was a pile of her books in the sitting room, just come that day. He'd ripped them to pieces. It was stupid and useless. They were easily replaceable and he'd still lose the house.

'I'd be prime suspect,' he said. 'They always know it's the husband.'

Feliks screwed up his eyes and leaned forward over the chess board.

'I'd do it for five thousand,' he said, staring his opponent hard in the eye.

Mike held his look, noting the grim sneer. He would do what Mike couldn't. Not simply ripping up her books, but her. It would be so convenient, thought Mike. He could grieve her passing, continue with Mandy on the sly, with the house wholly his. And her money too, he didn't know how much, but it was growing.

'I don't have five thou,' he said, breathing rapidly.

'How much have you got?' said Feliks putting the pieces back in the box.

'I'd need to look in my bank account.'

Feliks passed over his laptop. It was alive and waiting. Mike hesitated for a few seconds, then went into his account. Account number, password. A few clicks, and the screen was revealed.

'£3,726,' he said.

He looked at Feliks who was biting the side of his finger. Was it enough? He could sell a couple of guitars... What else did he have of value?

'Put it into my account,' said Feliks.

'All of it?'

'Every last penny.'

Mike chewed his lip as he looked at his computer page. His chin was itchy, he needed a shave. It was the only solution. Or leave Jean to clean him out.

'How will you do it?'

'I'm not telling you.'

Feliks had a faint smile. Was it an accusation of cowardice? The man was an operator, Mike was sure. Heaven knew what he'd done in his time. Mike was sweating, his neck prickly. Dare he? Dare he not?

'When will you do it?'

Feliks shook his head. 'Best you don't know.'

'Soon?' he said.

'A few days.' He held up his empty hands. 'I'll be no more specific. Just, it will be done. And you'll have no lies to tell.'

Mike imagined himself in the house, walking from room to room. All his. No one to come rushing in, screeching and pulling hair. Upstairs, downstairs, every towel and duvet. Jean had money coming into her bank account every day. And the car she'd bought only three months ago. It would be his. No more cutting comments, no more of that judgemental face. What would he do with Lily?

Think about her later. A trifle.

He looked up. Feliks was holding out his hand. Mike took it. And they shook.

'Give me your bank account details.'

Chapter 15

They had parked the car first of all and walked back to the supermarket en famille. Then picked up food for supper, and breakfast for him and Mia tomorrow. And his own lunch. At the last moment, even while at the till, he recalled the washing up liquid, and rushed back to get it.

She is so easy to be with, Jack thought. He couldn't stop looking at her and at Mia too, so obviously happy in their company. Was this the illusion? The future obscured in the cloud of a new relationship. No talk of money, no criticisms, no jostling in each other's spaces. He dismissed the thought. It was getting them married when they'd barely met.

Back home, Jack suggested that he and Jean do the cooking. Some time together at least in the kitchen.

'No, no,' exclaimed Mia. 'You'll be all schmaltzy, you two. Then it'll never get done. Me and Jean will do it.'

Jack accepted the truth of it, realising there was competition for Jean. And he'd lost. Kids. They get in the way. He felt resentful, hearing them through the kitchen door, Mia's shrill laughter, her softer voice. They were getting on, not unimportant. But...

How do you get rid of the kids?

He instantly felt guilty as Lily brought him Maurice Sendak's 'In the Night Kitchen' that Jean had had in her big bag. He settled on the sofa with her. We all have needs. The desire to be warmed and attended to. He wasn't doing so badly. But...

No 'but'. Mia and Jean were getting on. How dare he complain?

Jack read the tale as Lily turned the pages. She seemed to know all the words and when each page was done. Lily intrigued him, obviously knowing the words but refusing to say them. At what point would she switch on?

It was a weird tale, his mind only half on it, wondering what the three year old made of it. He suspected she liked the rhythm; perhaps it was like music, a familiar tune. The story hardly made sense. Well, not to him anyway.

He'd read the picture book three times before the food came. It was margherita pizza to which they'd added olives, red peppers, bits of walnut and pineapple pieces. They drank apple juice. Ice cream was to follow.

Jean cut off a small slice of pizza for Lily and trisected the remainder. She chopped up Lily's into small pieces.

'The best photos,' said Mia, 'are those with the conjunction over the streetlights and treetops. Otherwise it's just two tiddly stars in the sky.'

'They show where you are taking it from,' said Jean. 'Make it meaningful.'

'That's true,' said Mia thoughtfully. 'I want to download the best ones and send them to my school account.'

'You've still got homework to do,' said Jack.

'Oh Dad,' sighed Mia, rolling her eyes. 'Just like Mum. Can't I have any fun?'

'I'll help you,' said Jean.

Mia settled for that. And I'm the childminder, thought Jack. But at least Jean's here, and gets on with Mia. He couldn't have Jean to himself, not in this small flat, with the added demands of Lily and Mia.

Jean said, 'I'm not going home tonight. Not with Mike the way he was. It's not safe.'

Jack considered the possibility of her staying here. He only had one bedroom. When Mia stayed, he slept on the couch. Should he offer?

'You can stay here,' said Mia. 'Me, Jean and Lily can have the bedroom. Dad can sleep on the sofa.'

Jean flashed her hands. 'I can't do that to you. I was thinking of a hotel.'

'Stay,' said Jack. 'Sort yourself out tomorrow.'

Chapter 16

The morning was a bustle; the head of the queue for the bathroom was grabbed by Mia. Jack made tea. The small flat was like one of those crowded holiday lets where everyone mucks in, or it's chaos. Jean and Mia had opted to cook breakfast, leaving Jack to do the dirty dishes. He could smell the bacon, hear laughter and chatter. This was going to be better than his usual rush job.

Lily was drawing on a scrap of paper. Music was playing in the background, as Jack drank his second cup of tea, somewhat sleepy-eyed. In the early hours, he'd woken and couldn't get back to sleep. It was the worst time of night, the post midnight drag when alcohol croons its siren song. He must go back to Alcohol Halt, not simply now and again, but regularly. Learn how to deal with such times.

Jean came out of the bedroom a little later with Lily to go to the bathroom. On the way back, he'd asked her to stay, and the three cuddled up in his duvet. Lily fell asleep between them and they'd held each other, talked a little about children, the future. And Mike.

'I can't live in my own house,' she'd said. 'Do you know a good hit-man?'

Jack had suggested dropping a brick from the scaffolding tower, but saw she was somewhat more serious. How serious he couldn't fathom. He'd never wanted to kill Alison. Unless drunkenness filled in for murder. Besides, his ex had kicked him out, so there wasn't competition for space. The only death on offer was his own.

Lily and Jean had gone back to the bedroom and the worst was over for Jack. It was, though, another hour before he'd got to sleep. And seemed next to no time when his alarm was ringing. The clock he always put across the room, forcing him to get up to stop its jangle.

He yawned as Lily brought him over a picture to inspect. He praised it, knowing that's what you offer to the unrecognisable scribbles of three year olds. And quite quickly she brought him some more. A song was playing on the radio, Pink singing *Sober*. About the party being over. *How do I feel this good sober?* Except he was alright this morning. Breakfast was coming and there was work to do.

He must learn to deal with the early hours.

Breakfast was a feast. Eggs and bacon, fried bread, toast and marmalade and tea. Mia was chirpy, much better than she usually was in the morning. He thought again, this is a family. It wasn't of course, and it was. Or could be. He and Jean caught each other's eye. She smiled and he wondered whether she was thinking the same. Or simply smiling at him smiling at her.

Jean said, 'I have an idea I'd like to sound out.' Jack and Mia turned to her. 'I could work here. This place,' she added. 'You're out all day, Jack. It's not far from where I live.'

'Bit untidy,' said Jack.

'Soon remedied,' she shrugged, 'a run around with the vacuum cleaner, a few full bin bags. I can't concentrate at home. Every time he comes in I'm trembling. And when he's not there I'm wondering how long I've got before he's back. What do you think?'

Mia turned to Jack. 'Could work,' she said. 'Be nice to have someone here when I get back from school.'

'Have a go, see if it works for you,' said Jack, wondering what problems there might be, but welcoming her presence in his space.

'I'll go home this morning, get clean clothes for me and Lily. Then I must do some work. In the afternoon, I'm going to find Lily a childminder,' said Jean. He could see she was in business mode. 'I usually meet up with Maggie, a fellow writer, to do writerly and marketing things together. But I'll cancel her. She'll understand. And if I can get Lily sorted out, then maybe tomorrow I could come here?'

'Fine,' he said, trying to suppress his eagerness. She'd be here, the flat would get a spring clean. They were bound to meet every day. What was there to go wrong?

Chapter 17

Breakfast over, Jack was obligated to wash the dishes. That was the way it worked, at the holiday let. One party made the meal, the other cleared up afterwards.

He balked somewhat at the pile in the kitchen. Just about every plate he had, two frying pans, mugs from this morning and last night, and assorted utensils. But at least he wouldn't have to use window wash, and his client was here, and wouldn't complain if he was late on site.

Jean offered to run Mia to school. Mia took it up; she'd be in early but had some homework to finish off and wanted to check her photos had arrived. Jean came in the kitchen to say goodbye.

'I'll see you back at the house,' she said. 'I just hope Mike's temper is better today and he'll take Lily, so I can get some work done this morning. Then, it's operation childminder.'

They embraced, a long kiss until caught by Mia.

'Oi, you two! That's not how you do the dishes.'

The three females left him. Quarter of an hour later, he left himself, walking to Clova Road and the house. The sky had clouded over since yesterday. Did it look like rain? He hoped not as that would kill his work. It would bring him back early, on future days, to find Jean in his flat. Would she welcome that? She might a few times, then she'd get irritated at being interrupted.

It might not be so easy sharing the flat. It would stay tidy. One positive. She'd be on site. Another one. But she might not welcome him. Big negative.

At the house, he was reassured; his van was still there with no signs of entry. No one had come in the night to steal the tower or the block and tackle. He opened the garden door, having that key as well as the front door one. He climbed the tower, checking the tightness of the joints as he went up. They were fine, but he mustn't forget. It was his neck, and he only had one.

At the top, he looked at yesterday's work. The mortar was setting well in the pointing. Fine. Today's plan was to move the tower along, as it was best to work from the top of the wall down, so any splattering was underneath and could be cleaned off as you worked downwards.

The first problem was moving the scaffolding tower. A fence post was in the way. The tower would have to be dismantled and set up in the new position. Well, Feliks had forced him to pay for the privilege of being a few feet in his yard, but had said he'd assist him moving the tower. Now to see if the Pole kept his word.

Feliks was already at work. And from the condition of his hands and the smears on his face, had been working some time. The cement mixer was chugging away.

Feliks scowled when Jack asked for his help.

'You agreed,' insisted Jack.

'I didn't think it'd be every day. I need to put the rate up.'

'A deal is a deal,' said Jack. 'It'll only take the two of us ten minutes. It'll take longer standing here arguing.'

Feliks reluctantly conceded.

They worked from the top. Jack taking down the elements, passing them to Feliks who was down a level on the boards. Jack then clambered down to the level below him and took them from the Pole who then went down to ground level for the final dismantling.

Once in bits, they moved beyond the fence post to where the tower would be assembled, and did the action in reverse. Jack was impressed that Feliks knew exactly where to be, and tightened the fittings in his reach as they went up.

With the tower up, he helped Jack untangle the block and

tackle. The two of them stretching it along the house wall, to make it easier getting the tangles out of the rope.

'Did you go out on the razzle last night?' said Feliks with a sly nudge.

Jack was surprised at the Pole's use of idiom and wondered where he'd picked it up.

'My daughter was round last night,' he said, having no wish to say who else was present.

'I had a date,' said the Pole and kissed his fingers. 'Classy woman. We went to an Indian restaurant in Stratford. You know the Himalaya?'

'I do. On the way to Maryland.'

'Intelligent woman. A head teacher. She lives round here.'

Jack had an inkling who it might be, though couldn't be sure.

'How did you make out? he said.

'All in hand,' he said, pressing an index finger and thumb together to indicate satisfaction. 'The classy ones take two nights. The scrubbers first night. But the classy ones, you don't want them thinking you are only after one thing.' He chuckled. 'I tell them I want a family life. Someone to share the future with.' He punched Jack lightly on the shoulder. 'You know the way it goes.'

Jack thought, if it's Alison, she'll be asking me to look after Mia again. But he wouldn't, not tonight. He had his own fish to fry.

Chapter 18

Jean drove up the road, past her house, looking for a parking space. She'd taken Mia to school and they'd had a bit of a chat. So good to get on with her, as a relationship could never work if she was against it. But she mustn't run ahead of herself. There was Mike to be dealt with.

There was Jack's van with his Jack of All Trades logo. She had to drive on further. This was such a pain. There was talk of a residents' parking plan, but that could be years away. Now she had the money, she could take down the front garden wall and pave it over for a drive. For weeks she'd thought that, every time she drove up and down this road looking for somewhere to put the car. Then promptly forgot it as work, Lily, and Mike took over.

Always back to Mike. She'd perhaps talk to Jack about making a drive. But first Mike. He was one, two and three in her priorities. Jettison him. He took her over, and she hated it. That useless weed smoking, cleaner-shagging slob. Get him out of her head.

Out of her house.

Such a state she was in this morning, just going home. And of course, he'd be there. How would he react, she wondered, as she and Lily came in? The last she'd seen of him had been that fearful row. At least there were people about now, some protection, she thought seeing Jack and Feliks assembling the tower as she approached. The sections passing from one to the other, up and up, almost like a dance. She stopped to watch, pointing it out to Lily, the pieces going from Jack up to Feliks. And then a level was done, the higher of the two, Feliks climbing up to the next, while Jack went up a level to pass the elements up.

She wanted a wave from Jack, but didn't wish to call out, not with Feliks there. Mustn't be too needy, or too revealing for that matter. She had to face Mike.

She took Lily's hand and went to the front door, standing there a little while, thinking out the possibilities. Mike might not be in, or he might be in and be sullen and unpredictable. Oh dear, she shouldn't have to come home to this. Above all, she must not antagonise him. Yesterday, she had flared up too easily. Not smart.

Think for Lily, as well as herself.

She was perhaps a minute at the door, then berated herself for inaction. This was her house. She had every right to be in it. She mustn't cower; he would see it and he would use it. Jean took a deep breath and opened the front door. She would find him straightaway, and work out their terms of reference. But she had no need to search, for immediately the front door closed, Mike was out of the sitting room to greet her.

'Hello,' she said cautiously.

'I'm sorry about yesterday,' he said.

He was bleary-eyed, wearing an un-ironed shirt. She wondered if he'd slept here last night, but wasn't going to ask. That was no longer her business.

She said, 'We can't have another day like yesterday.'

'I agree.'

'Oh.' She was a little taken aback by his acquiescence.

'Let's have a coffee,' he said. 'I've made some.'

'You're not going to talk me into calling off the divorce?'

He waved his hands. 'No, I accept we are on that road. Just...' he hesitated, then went on, 'we need to work out the rules. For Lily's sake.'

She remained wary, although he seemed to be going her way. It was the drugs he took that made him a monster. Sometimes, he was quite civilised.

'I'll have a coffee then,' she said.

They went into the kitchen. It was too tidy. She knew he hadn't been here last night. Neither of them had. She guessed where he'd been. She would say as little as possible about her own travels.

Mike had already made coffee. He was preparing for this, she thought. She'd better listen and keep her cool. Don't criticise.

Mike poured them both a coffee from the cafetiere. He gave Lily some juice. They sat at the table, almost like strangers. A lot had happened to both of them in twenty four hours.

'You didn't stay here last night,' he said. 'Did you?'

'I was at a friend's. I didn't trust staying in the house with you.'

He was silent a while. And she thought, this is all very well, this niceness, but what about when you're drugged up. Who am I facing then?

'I behaved very badly,' he said. 'I apologise completely.'

'I do too,' she said, half unsure what she was apologising for, but felt she had to come towards him.

'We have to work together on this. For Lily's sake.'

'Yes,' she said. But didn't believe him. This was the man who had been sleeping with the cleaner for god knows how many months. Who was dealing and smoking so much himself that he couldn't even look for a job. But regardless of his demerits, she and Lily had to stay safe. What he did with whom was none of her business anymore. And vice versa. Get the rules right. She didn't want to be in the firing line of another pickle jar.

'I'll take Lily today,' he said.

'That's kind of you,' she said, wondering what he was up to. This was too easy. There had to be something behind these pleasantries.

'I know you need to work,' he said. 'And this afternoon you have your regular scene with what's her name.'

'Maggie,' she said. Her cancellation of the meeting with Maggie was none of his business. And fixing up a childminder would only be, if she were able to settle it.

'I've got to go up to Stratford this morning and do some shopping...' he said.

'I don't want you taking Lily with you when you do your drug deals,' she retorted.

'I'm going shopping,' he said fiercely. 'I do buy other things. What do you think of me?' He sighed. 'I need some underwear, a set of guitar strings, and a couple of flash drives.'

Maybe, she thought. Though what could she prove? Just get him out of the house, away from herself and Lily. In the meantime, get a childminder.

'Then Lily and I will go off and see my mother in Romford for the afternoon,' he added.

'That all sounds fine,' she said agreeably. 'Perhaps we should have a coffee every morning and work out the day.'

'Good idea,' said Mike.

They were silent. Business done. What else did they have to say to each other? There were too many topics that could rekindle the war.

She said, 'I'll get Lily washed and changed. And then she's all yours for the day.' Adding as an afterthought, 'Thank you for being so considerate.'

'Don't mention it.'

Chapter 19

At the front of the house, Jack was on his knees, trowelling sand into a bucket, which already contained cement which he'd put in when he'd got his tools from the shed, as it was one less journey. He'd have enough of them with all the up and down on the tower. Jack's mortar mix was one part cement to three parts sand and a dollop of plasticizer to half a bucket of mix. A higher proportion of cement than a regular mortar mix for bricklaying, but he'd been given the pointing recipe by an old hand. He'd asked the old bricklayer how much a dollop was, to be told 'a bit more than a splash'. It reminded Jack of his mother's cooking: a pinch of this, a lump of that.

He didn't need the mix now, but had it ready for the afternoon when he'd do the pointing. This morning he was going to be chipping out mortar.

Mike and Lily came out of the house. The instant Jack saw him, he wished he hadn't been trying to be so efficient. He could so easily have been up the top of the tower, chipping away, with no chance of an encounter. Too late for alternatives, he must try to behave naturally, like any regular builder on a job. He hadn't actually screwed Mike's missus last night, though he'd got mightily close. It was only children that halted the activity.

'Morning,' he said, with an attempt at a smile.

Mike and Lily came over. Jack was still on his knees, the bucket by his side, next to the huge sack of sand.

'How's it going, mate?' asked Mike.

'Good start yesterday,' said Jack indicating the area under the eaves that he'd pointed. 'I've moved the tower this morning and will do another section today. If the weather holds.'

Lily detached herself from Mike and threw her arms round Jack's neck.

'Yack,' she said.

'Was that a word?' said Mike. 'You're especially favoured, if so. Her very first.'

'You left her with me yesterday morning,' said Jack awkwardly, eager to explain the affection. 'Before the fracas...'

Mike gave a half laugh. 'Sorry about all that, mate.' He tapped him on the shoulder. 'She caught me in the act.'

'I mind my own business,' said Jack with a shrug. 'I'm just here to point your walls.'

Only half true, but it was what one should say in the circumstance. He rose, bringing Lily up with him. He placed her on the ground and she took his hand.

'Jean's mad at me still,' said Mike, flapping a hand, as if it were a slight tiff.

'These things happen,' said Jack, not wanting to get drawn further.

'She's talking of divorce.' He tutted. 'You know what women are like. One fling and they go wild. But it'll blow over, I'm sure.'

'Bound to,' said Jack. 'Where you off to?' Anything to change the subject.

'Out all day,' said Mike. 'Getting odds and ends in Stratford, then away to see my mum in Romford.' He smiled brightly. 'She likes to see Lily. I can leave the two of 'em together and have a drink with an old mate of mine. He's got a stall in the market.'

'I had a girlfriend in Romford once,' said Jack. Why did he say that? He hadn't thought of her in ages. Talk, any words, to get him away from the topic of Jean.

'Must be going,' said Mike. 'Keep an eye on the old lady

for me.' He leaned forward mock confidentially, 'Make sure she doesn't shag the postman.' He laughed.

Jack tried hard for a grin. Lily didn't want to let go of his hand.

'Come on, luvey. I'll buy you some sweeties.'

She let go reluctantly, bribery working for an instant, but she didn't have the sweets and came back to Jack. Impatiently, Mike lifted her away, rolling his eyes.

'Jack'll be here later,' he said. 'Let's go get those sweeties.'

And he carried her off over his shoulder, Lily's hands stretching back to Jack. He gave her a wave, and the two of them left him. He was sweating round the neckband. Such a lousy liar, what with Lily there holding his hand... Had she said his name? Or was it just a sound? If she were talking, she might easily have dropped him in it. Told Daddy where Mummy was last night, and who she was kissing.

Best to avoid Mike, if he could, for the rest of the job. It was coming out here for the sand that forced the meeting. He needn't have done. But how was he to know Mike would come out at that instant? Bound to happen though. Jack would have to get used to it, the husband around. Not working. Stoned half the time. Talk football to him. Music, the guy was into that. Get him on the artists he liked. Any subject but his wife.

Anyway, Mike was off for the day. Good riddance.

A youngish Asian man had gone next door. Another of Saffron's punters, he guessed. Respectable, in a light blue suit. A sharp dresser. Getting a quickie perhaps, before going on to the bank. He kept half an eye on him as he trowelled in sand. Saffron opened the door in a short dressing gown, revealing a lot of leg and plump thigh. The lady had all sorts. He'd seen them come and go. Black, white, mostly older than this guy. Obviously Feliks didn't object. She must pay her rent on time. And knowing him, he charged her over the odds.

The door closed, and the man left. Not a punter, or she was too pricy for him. He came down the steps and down the path. On the pavement, the young man hesitated. It was there that Jack recognised him.

He stood up and waved an arm. 'Fayyad!'

The man looked about, perplexed as to where the cry came from. Then saw Jack beckoning him over. He strode to where Jack was working. Jack was sure now. It was him. Clean shaven, his dark brown hair neat and short.

'Do I know you?' he said, his face screwed in puzzlement.

Jack smiled broadly. 'You sure do, mate. Though I may have changed a bit. Jack Bell.'

The man broke into a grin and snapped his fingers. 'Bloody hell, man. Must be fifteen years.' He held out his hand.

Jack took it and they shook. 'You're looking respectable,' he said. 'Last time I saw you, you were working on a clothing stall in Queen's Market.'

Fayyad waved a hand in dismissal. 'Don't remind me. My uncle's. What a bossy ape he was. The slightest thing I did wrong he'd tell my dad. I couldn't get away from there fast enough.' He looked Jack up and down in his overalls. 'You working here?'

'Yeh. I'm a builder. You might've seen my van up the road.'

'Jack of All Trades!' He burst out laughing. 'I should've guessed. You making a living?'

'Getting by. This job should last me six weeks. And yourself?'

'What do you think?' Fayyad stood up straight, indicating his suit, white shirt and tie.

'A banker or estate agent,' guessed Jack. When his friend shook his head, he said, 'An agent for an energy company, a charity chugger...' He stopped. 'Come on. Tell me.'

'I'm a cop.'

Jack took a step back and looked him over. 'I can see you're not a hod carrier. But a cop? I'd never have guessed.'

'Detective Constable Kamani,' he said proudly. 'I was in uniform up to last week. This is my first day in mufti.'

'So what's a detective doing here?'

'The old lady next door.' He indicated Feliks' house. 'She's disappeared. Mrs Jackson. I'm here to talk to the neighbours.' Then added quietly, 'Could be nothing. That's why they sent the new boy. She might turn up tomorrow. But it's a couple of days since anyone's seen her.'

Jack said, 'I broke into her house.' Adding with a short laugh, 'All legal, guv'nor. Her landlord and son didn't have a key, so they asked me to get in.'

'So we'll find your prints all over her flat.' He wrinkled his nose. 'A suspect. A dodgy builder...'

'Put away the handcuffs,' laughed Jack.

Fayyad chuckled. 'Good to see you looking well. I saw Bob, maybe two years ago. He said you were in some sort of trouble...'

'Yeh,' said Jack uncomfortably. 'Drink. Ended my marriage. I was on the streets for a couple of weeks.' He stopped, this wasn't the time for life stories. 'That's all over. I'm a builder. Clean.'

Fayyad patted him on the shoulder. 'Glad to hear that, Jack. I'm married myself. Two kids, living in Ilford. You must come up and see us.'

'I'd love to.'

'And maybe you can help me here.' He was looking at the two houses. 'Who do I need to talk to?'

'There's Saffron and Feliks in that house. The old lady lives downstairs in the basement flat. Saffron, who you just saw, is a prostitute...' And stopped. Maybe he shouldn't have said that to a cop.

'No wonder she wanted to get rid of me. Where's the landlord?'

'Feliks. He's in his garden, working on his shed. You want me to take you to him?'

'If you would, Jack.'

Jack led him through the garden gate, along where the fencing had been taken down for the scaffolding tower. Crossing to the other garden, keeping to the path, they walked by the lawn and vegetable patch to where Feliks was shovelling cement into his mixer. He looked up, shovel in hand, as the two approached.

'Detective Constable Fayyad Kamani wants a word,' said Jack.

'What about?' His weather beaten face creased in irritation.

'About Mrs Jackson,' said Fayyad. 'Her son has reported her missing.'

'I'll leave you,' said Jack.

'Thanks, mate,' said Fayyad. 'Catch you later.'

Jack left them. Going down the garden, he turned back for an instant and saw Fayyad in professional mode, his notebook out to take notes. Fancy meeting him. They'd been at Cumberland School together. Useless school, well useless for Jack anyway. Maybe if he'd worked... He'd always liked Fayyad. Good cricketer. He remembered being clean bowled by him. A cop! He'd never have guessed.

Jack brought the bucket in and left it by the tap on the patio for when he wanted to add the water, well away from where he'd be chipping out old mortar. He climbed up the scaffolding, his phone ringing when he was midway up. He wasn't going to answer on a ladder, and let it ring.

He got to the top, just in time to answer. It was Alison. Would he get anything done today?

'Hello, Jack?'

'How did your date go?' he said. Might as well find out if he was right.

'Oh, what a charming man! We went to the Himalaya. Do you know it?'

'I do. On the way to Maryland.' Her date had to be Feliks. He could warn her off, but she wouldn't welcome his advice.

'Did you end up in bed?' he said, to double check.

'Not everyone's like you, Jack,' she admonished. 'We're both looking for commitment.'

'And I'm not?'

'I don't know anymore.'

He was, sort of. Though he'd take a one night stand if it was on offer.

'So what's this call in aid of?' he said, knowing every Alison call had a purpose.

'Can you do me a big favour and take Mia again tonight?'

'Sorry,' he said. 'But I've a date tonight.' He hadn't. Not yet.

She sighed. 'I was hoping you'd be available. He's got tickets for the Theatre Royal... I shall have to try Moira. Enjoy your date.' She ended the call abruptly.

Well, he was no use to her. That was close to rude. He pictured her in her office. Well paid, phoning around for childcare on school money. But he shouldn't gripe. What was he doing, but talking to old mates and his ex – and not earning a penny. He began working, scraping out old mortar with a plugging chisel. It came out easily enough, too easily, as he'd learnt yesterday. It was likely this brickwork hadn't ever been pointed. Most likely original mortar, dating back to the 1880s.

All around here had been farmland. Owned by the Gurneys, Elizabeth Fry's family. One of the few things he remembered from school, walking the boundary of their estate with clipboards. Then the railway came and the developers followed them. First generation houses, these.

How long would his mortar last? If he did a decent job, it would see him out.

His contemplation of history didn't last long. Back to Jean. He'd invite her over to his place. Without kids. She was

107

at home, he was pretty sure. Lily was out with Mike, going to his mother. And Jean had said she was going to be busy this morning. Best not interrupt. He'd catch her at lunchtime, and hope he could fix up the evening.

Then Alison could ask him how it had gone.

Chapter 20

Mandy and Mike were smoking a spliff. Lily was on the swings and Mike was idly pushing her. Two Asian women had left them to it, perhaps recognising the smell of the burning herb.

Mandy sat on an adjoining swing with the joint, pushing idly back and forth. She took a deep draw, and held in the puff as long as she could while lying back on the swing, before slowly exhaling, feeling pleasantly woozy as the swing lifted.

'So what was the bitch like this morning?' she said haltingly, a smile filling her face as she took down the smoke.

'We've declared a truce,' he said. 'Or at least she thinks I have. Pass the spliff.'

Mandy stopped her swing and handed it over. Mike took a drag.

'So what are you planning, smarty pants?' she said.

'Some things are better for you not to know,' he said, and laughed as a vision caught him. He was walking round the empty house in bare feet. There was no sign of her. Not a dress or pair of shoes, the bathroom cleared of her smellies, no hats or coats, no piles of paper or her books.

'You're not planning to bump her off. Are you?'

His smile ceased. Mandy was sharp.

'Of course not,' he said, which was a half truth as he had no plans in that direction himself. He'd subcontracted the work.

'She'll get everything,' she said. 'I know her sort. Cut your dick off, if she could.'

'We'll see,' he said cheerily. 'I've got one or two things in the wind. Don't you worry, girl. The troubles of today are sufficient thereof.' His grin was bubbling over as he tapped his temple. 'Something still in there from Sunday school. In the beginning was the word... '

'You're stoned,' she said.

'Best way to start the day.'

He stood over her swing and kissed her. She clutched him to her, oblivious of others in the playground watching the pair, her hands massaging the cheeks of his bum.

Lily's swing had stopped. She protested. Mike reluctantly drew away from Mandy, and half stumbling and laughing, he gave his daughter a push.

'My old lady, the famous writer of suspense fantasy, never read one myself, better things to do... The big hoot'll be out all afternoon at Maggie's. Two tarts talking about marketing and plots and how to string me up by the goolies.' He laughed. 'While I'll be at my mother's eating fruit cake and drinking Tetley's. So the house is all yours, sweetheart. Just make sure you keep out of the way of the builder.'

'I want my shoe back,' she said. 'I'll take my time. And see what else she's got.'

'Have a good look, plenty of time.'

And he went back to pushing Lily. He had considered calling this opportunity for robbery off. After all, pretty soon, all her stuff would be his. But calling it off would require explanation, and best if only Feliks and he knew about their agreement. Then Mandy couldn't get caught out. Besides which, once Jean was gone, he'd help Mandy out anyway. So let her have a little in advance.

'Want Yack!' declared Lily.

'Did you hear that?' exclaimed Mike. 'Two words. And not about me who's been doing most of the caring, but some builder who had her for ten minutes...'

'Until the flying banshee arrived and nearly clawed my

110

eyes out.' She passed Mike the joint and grasped the chains and pushed herself into the air, her long brown hair draping like a curtain as she lay back. 'She owes me, and I'll make sure I get well paid. Enough for a holiday and Christmas.'

'Don't overdo it,' he said, wondering whether he should tell her that things had changed. But he didn't want a scene. Let her have what she can get. 'It's cool,' he said, taking a long drag. 'Fill your bag at the free shop.'

After all, he was.

Chapter 21

Jack and Jean were having coffee in the kitchen. He'd worked for a couple of hours up top, skipped any tea break as he figured he'd had enough interruptions earlier. And been thinking of her, every scrape and chip. He was almost ready to quit for lunch when she'd called him down.

They'd embraced eagerly; he'd suggested going up to the bedroom. But she'd said she had a cop coming over in quarter of an hour. She'd fobbed the young detective off earlier, telling him she had work to finish.

While he drank coffee, Jean sorted out a cold lunch.

'I'll find time for you, darling,' she said. 'I promise.'

'How about this evening?' he said. 'Mia'll be with her mum.'

'Love to,' she said. 'Can you cook?'

'I can do what I'm told.'

'That might be useful,' she said slyly. 'In the kitchen or elsewhere. I'll bring some food over. You can chop vegetables?'

'Yes, captain.' He was pleased the date had been arranged. A night in together.

'I hope I can get Mike to have Lily this evening...' She was pulling out salad and cheeses from the fridge.

'How was he this morning?'

'Surprisingly civil. He's accepted the fact of a divorce. And promised to behave.'

'Do you believe him?'

'I don't know. It's hard to accept the turnaround. But then he's like that. Tomorrow he could be a monster again.'

'You could stay with me until this is sorted out.'

She looked at him, startled.

'You hardly know me, Jack.'

'I saw you with Mia last night,' he said. 'She really likes you.'

She laughed. 'So that's your criteria.'

'Yes,' he said. 'I get Mia to mark my girlfriends out of ten. Saves a lot of time.'

'So the conjunction of Venus and Jupiter was a test.'

'Which you passed.'

'You don't know what I'm like in bed.'

'You were pretty good on the sofa last night.'

'That was foreplay. I might be too demanding. How much can you take?'

'Put me to the test,' he said.

'I will. Most definitely.'

As she put out a bowl of salad, she kissed him on the forehead, and returned to the units for a plate of cheeses, a board of bread slices and the butter.

'Mike's well and truly sick of me,' she went on as she gave them both plates and cutlery. 'If I dropped down dead today, he'd dance on my grave. Help yourself.'

Jack took two slices of bread.

'Why do you think that is?' he said, as he buttered the bread.

'Because I'm too critical.' She spooned salad onto her plate. 'Because he doesn't like to be kept by me. Because he knows I can't stand slobs.' She looked at Jack keenly. 'Consider. With him out of the way, I might well turn on you. Like a hungry rottweiler.'

Holding her look, he said, 'I don't smoke weed, I work for a living. And I don't have a cleaner.'

She chuckled. 'I noticed that from the state of your flat. But you'll have me tomorrow. You won't recognise the place when you get home.'

He came round and kissed her. A long embrace, broken by a ring on the bell.

'The long arm of the law!' she exclaimed.

'He's an old mate of mine,' he said.

'Then he should have more consideration,' she said, breaking away. 'I'll see him in the sitting room. I'll be as quick as I can. You have your lunch.'

She left him.

Jack munched a cheese and lettuce sandwich. On his own again. But for Fayyad, they'd be upstairs in the bedroom. Still, it was arranged for this evening. So he shouldn't moan. Mia would be with Alison, or whoever she'd arranged for their daughter. Of course, Jean might have to bring Lily. He hoped not, but Mike would have had her all day and might rebel at having her for the night too. But if she came, it couldn't be helped. Toddlers sleep, sooner or later.

And he'd invited her to live with him. It had just come out. A mad thing to do, but they'd got on so well. So far. He thought of his early days with Alison. Young love. In some ways Jean was like her. Strong, ambitious. He suspected that was what attracted him to both of them. But Alison had in the end overwhelmed him. This felt different. He was older, more in control, and he was working. Of course, Jean earned more than he did. Probably lots more. Which could be a problem, or might not be. His skills were improving. He could take on bigger jobs in time. Earn more. Maybe he should find a partner, though working alone had its advantages. No one to argue with, or be cheated by.

Mia got on well with Jean. Always a prime consideration. She was always complaining about Alison's boyfriends. Though she complained less about his girlfriends, but then he held back from moving them in. And didn't keep them long. Either he was lousy with women, or unlucky. He preferred to think it was the latter. Besides, Jean was here, and plainly wanted him. Their relationship might last two weeks, or a lifetime.

The front door slammed and she returned.

'There wasn't much I could tell him,' she said as she sat down at the table. 'I haven't seen Mrs Jackson for three days. Don't know where she is. I know her to say hello to, hardly more. He's gone off to visit that prostitute...'

'Saffron.'

She chewed a spring onion. 'I wonder why men go to prostitutes.'

'Sex,' said Jack. 'And no demands.'

'It doesn't sound much fun,' she mused, putting cheese and tomato on a slice of bread. 'Not unless you pay lots. Have you ever been to one?'

'No.'

'I wonder whether Mike has visited her. It wouldn't surprise me. That's how you spread pox.' She laughed. 'Sorry. Not exactly lunchtime conversation.'

Jack visualised Saffron's big thighs and the number of men he'd seen going in and out. It made him queasy. You have to pretend you're the only one, not one of a long queue.

'Well, I had a good morning,' she said, crunching a lettuce leaf which she'd dipped in mayonnaise. 'I actually got some writing done. Post apocalyptic stuff with magic. Mia would like it. I'll go on with it at your place tomorrow, once I've vacuumed. I can't work in a mess.'

'It's not that bad,' Jack protested. Max had done it only two days ago.

'Depends who's looking,' she said. 'But I mustn't be ungrateful. It's small. And I'm fussy. I'll get it ship shape and I won't complain. After all, I am getting it free. Aren't I?'

'Yes.' He'd never thought of charging, especially if she might be moving in.

'Then my role is to keep it clean. Call it the rent. I'll buy you decent curtains too.'

'Might you move in?' he asked cautiously.

'Tempting,' she mused. 'It would get me out of Mike's

sphere while the divorce is going through. Let's talk it over this evening.' She looked at her watch. 'I've quarter of an hour to get to the first childminder. I've three lined up for this afternoon.' Adding mock forlornly, 'There are other things I'd much rather do, Jack. You do understand?'

'Of course,' he said. 'I know this is a rocky time.'

'I am an organiser,' she said, shaking her fists. 'Take care, I might organise you. But first myself. I can't do anything when I don't know whether I'm coming or going. And that means sorting out childminding, and getting my living and working space right.' She sighed. 'It's all a tumble at the moment, but I'll make time for you. I promise.'

Chapter 22

Mandy hid behind the car opposite Mike and Jean's house. In the vehicle's mirror, she could see the builder at the top of the scaffolding tower. He was helmeted, wearing safety goggles and knocking out the mortar from the brickwork just below the eaves. There was a splatter of chippings bouncing off the tower and hitting the ground. She watched him a while. Although concentrating on his work, he was half turned in her direction. And might be for some time.

He must not see her getting in the house.

After leaving the swings, she'd accompanied Mike and Lily to Stratford. Then gone home for an hour. It wouldn't do to come to the house too early. Or too late. She wanted to make the most of her time here. It would be empty, and she'd have at least three hours as Jean would be out all afternoon with her writer mate.

Times were rough. Acting was looking less likely. She needed money, and it was Jean, by rights, who should supply it. The cow had got her sacked. If it wasn't Mike's house too, she'd shit in the bed and scrawl her curses in faeces round the walls. But no, this was burglary. She must remember to leave a window open when she left, to show the apparent entry point.

Coming down the road earlier, she'd spotted Jean's car. It meant she was still at home. Unless she wasn't going to use it. Mandy had waited at the street corner and after about fifteen minutes saw her coming. She'd hid behind a lime tree, well out of sight, given her a few minutes, then had gone back. The car had gone.

Step one. Jean was away. Now she had to get by the builder unseen, and into the house.

Across the road from Jack, she crouched low behind the line of vehicles and rapidly traversed the house. Once out of his line of sight, she stood upright and continued down the road for about fifty metres. She then crossed over and walked rapidly up to the house.

She listened to the tell tale drip of chippings. If they stopped, she'd have to retreat. She must not be seen. She'd been sacked. The house was out of bounds for her. This had to appear a random burglary.

Mandy climbed over the low wall. Not using the gate, where she might be seen by the builder from his tower. She kept in close to the house, as she made her way to the steps. Then quietly up them, stopping in the relative safety of the portico. If Jack were to climb down now, she'd hear him and could be in the house before he got to ground level.

Looking behind warily, as if fearing a bogeyman might pounce, she opened the front door and stepped into the hallway. Then, slowly and gently, she shut the door.

She was in. Her heart pounding, she leaned against the wall by the row of hats and umbrellas. In the house and unseen. There would be the getting out when she'd done of course, which had its own difficulties, but worry about that when the time came. She was in. What a relief! And no one here for the afternoon but herself.

She had the added advantage of knowing the house. She'd been coming twice a week for a couple of years. Nominally for one hour, but post lovemaking she'd had to do some work – and so stayed longer. Over the period, Jean had put in a few complaints. Nothing that would have got her fired, that is, until yesterday.

Surprising their luck had held so long. She'd always known that one day Jean was going to walk in on them. Just hoped it would always be in the future.

Mandy went into the sitting room. Nothing much of interest in there. A few vases, too big really. Her loot had to be small, valuable things that she could take away in her backpack. She went into the kitchen. She was peckish; she hadn't much at home. Mandy mooched around the fridge, taking some salad and cheese. Not bothering with a plate, she'd only have to wash it up.

In her chaotic planning, she'd considered wearing rubber gloves, but knew her fingerprints would be all over the house anyway. There wasn't one room she hadn't cleaned many times, if somewhat haphazardly.

She went upstairs.

Chapter 23

Jean was annoyed. This was becoming tedious. There was nowhere to park on her road. Who did all these vehicles belong to? Couldn't simply be the residents. Though quite a few of the houses had multiple tenancies, she reflected. So maybe they were.

She drove down to the end, gave up, and turned down a side street. There she found a spot, perhaps two hundred metres from the house. It was ridiculous. The childminder had not even been half a mile away. She could've walked there. It would've been less hassle. Except she thought she'd be going to see three, but the first one was so well set up, so organised, that why bother with the other two? The woman who opened the door was an intelligent, middle aged woman; there was a play room, toys in the garden, bookshelves with a range of picture books. The woman said she never had the TV on and they went to the park every day.

The car at last parked, before quitting the vehicle, Jean phoned to cancel the two other appointments. She was to the point but polite, apologising but saying she had now made other arrangements, without going into detail. She was pleased with herself, no longer dependent on Mike's vagaries. The plan now was to get him out of the house. Though he had no money. Let him go live with the cleaner. Love in a garret, he was welcome to it. Might take some time though.

She could try bribery.

Jean picked up her light brown half-length coat and left the vehicle. Outside she straightened the coat, doing up the black buttons. She'd always liked this coat. It was smart and comfortable, and she knew it suited her. She locked up and headed for the house. Some enforced exercise, the walk. She was getting lax, though she had a cycle machine in her workroom. Good intentions gone to pot. She must get back to using it. Could she take it to Jack's, that is if she moved in? His flat was small, though. Or perhaps she should go for a run every day.

When? First thing or after a morning's writing? First thing was more efficient. Out of bed, into her running gear, out the house and jogging. Fifteen minutes or so round the houses, only one shower needed. But that regime was quite monastic, especially when sleeping with someone new.

Or what about a bike? One of those folding Bromptons. That'd be good. It would have worked with her three interviews, none were far away. Whatever she did, she needed an exercise programme, or she wouldn't keep it up. But then her whole life needed a programme. A plan, taking into account childminding, exercise, her writing, her online courses and her personal time. She should stop watching TV for a start, that really drained the hours. She'd like to get rid of the set, but Mike watched it endlessly, god knows what. And if she moved to Jack's, she couldn't make any demands. Would moving in with him work out?

Temporarily, it would remove her from the problem of Mike. Especially if he wouldn't go. He was such a slob. Jack's place would be OK for a few weeks. Too small for any longer. Though, once the divorce was through, she could move back in to the house. And if her relationship was still going with Jack, he was such a genuine guy, then they could either keep up both places, people often did these days, or he could move in with her. Dangers there, but Mia was a delight. It just could work.

Options, options. But at least the childminder kept her in control.

Suppose she paid Mike off. Gave him, say twenty five

thou, on the agreement he moved out and didn't come back. It would have to be done with a solicitor or she'd have no comeback if he welshed on it. Give it to him in instalments while the divorce was going through.

A plan forming. She'd have to sort out the detail, but she'd so love to get Mike out of her life.

She was at the house. And realised the walk had helped her think things through. It wasn't a waste of time. You couldn't sort your head out while driving, or at least not around here with all the impatient drivers on the road, half of them on their mobiles or smoking, one hand on the wheel. You had to be ready for anything.

Jack was up on the tower, chippings pattering down.

She called to him. 'Jack!'

He stopped working, looked down and waved. 'You're back early.'

She mimed drinking. 'Coffee?'

'Love one.'

He put down his tools and climbed down the tower.

They didn't make it as far as the kitchen but were diverted to the bedroom.

Chapter 24

The front door slammed, jolting Mandy. She was upstairs in the bedroom deciding what to add to her loot. Couldn't be Mike as she'd gone with him and Lily to the train station. So had to be Jean, back early for some reason. The cow was always doing that. Unlikely she'd come straight up here. Probably make herself a coffee. Mike said she lived on coffee. If so, Mandy could sneak out while she was in the kitchen.

A jettisoned thought, as footsteps ran up the stairs. Mandy just had time to slide under the bed, as the door swung wide in excited voices and laughter, and two bodies flung themselves on the bed. The mattress rocked and rolled and clothing was tossed over the sides.

She knew one of the bodies was Jean, the other she wasn't sure of, until boots and overalls told her it was the builder. Quite a surprise; shagging the builder, the hypocritical bitch. Jean's shoes hit the floor, followed by tights, blouse, bra, his socks, shirt, vest and pants, scattered all about the bed like litter after a pop festival.

There was little conversation, mostly bounce and rolling, the odd endearment, gasping. The bedroom door was open. Mandy wondered whether they would see her if she crawled to it. And then she saw her backpack, in clear view, leaning against the dressing table. One look inside would be a total giveaway: Jean's laptop and jewellery. There was no good explanation for those items. And with them her own phone and purse to completely identify her as the thief. Stupid, dead dog stupid. But Mike, bloody Mike, had insisted Jean would be out all afternoon.

She'd have to sit it out, and find a way to get her backpack.

Chapter 25

Feliks was shovelling stones into the concrete mixer. With luck, he could finish today, and get the machine back early before another day could be charged. Depending, though, what that teacher was doing. He'd foolishly bought the tickets for the Theatre Royal, forgetting she had a daughter. He could return them and get his money back, if he did it early enough.

He put down the shovel, his hands smeared with cement and sand. And unscrewed the cup on his thermos and poured himself a coffee. Barely warm. He drank it in one and screwed the cup back on. He scratched his groin. The advantages of Saffron on tap were no foreplay to mess with. No need to satisfy a whore. No complaints. And straight back to work.

Then again, he enjoyed seduction. The challenge of it. Sussing out a woman, finding out what she wanted and being her dream lover. The teacher wanted a family life, then so did he. She liked movies and theatre. So did he. She liked holidays off the tourist trail. And strangely enough, so did he.

His pager rang. An ancient thing; he'd bought it amongst a job lot at an auction. Ringing was sufficient for its purpose. He switched it off and rubbed his hands down his gritty jeans, spreading rather than removing the dirt, and headed for the house.

Two birds with one stone.

He passed the vegetable patch, noting the brussels sprouts he'd planted out in June, not doing badly, a few beans on the bean poles. He'd need to pick the remaining corn cobs. To the back door of the house. Quietly, he opened up and closed the door after him. Then picked up the old pickaxe handle in the corner by the door. It pleased him to reuse rather than throw out.

And he walked without sound down the hallway. At Saffron's door, he switched mode, pushing open the door, crossed the sitting room and strode into the bedroom.

He smashed the half dressed punter across the face with the pickaxe handle. The middle aged man gasped and fell back on the bed. Feliks crossed the space between them and hauled the man up by his sparse hair as he spat out a tooth, blood dribbling down his lips.

'You come, you pay,' shouted Feliks into his face.

He released the man who sank on to the bed groaning. Feliks pulled the wallet from the man's trousers on the floor. He threw it to Saffron. She was naked below her black bra, her eyes almost shut. The pea brained tart was stoned again.

'How much has he got?' he said.

Saffron opened the wallet, took out the notes and began counting them. No wonder the man didn't want to pay when she was in that state.

'Get up!' he commanded the punter.

The man stumbled to his feet, groaning, and said some words that Feliks recognised as Russian. If he'd known he'd have hit him twice as hard. Feliks gathered up the man's clothing and thrust the items into his arms. On top, he placed the man's thinner wallet.

'On your way, Russkie!'

He pushed him out of the bedroom, into the sitting room. Continuing to propel him, he thrust him out the flat door and into the hallway.

'Go back to Moscow!'

Leaving him there, Feliks withdrew into the flat. Saffron had come out of the bedroom and had put on a short dressing gown. She was clutching a bundle of notes.

'120 pounds,' she said.

He grasped them from her and thrust them into his jeans

pocket. She put out a feeble hand for her share. He slapped her round the face.

'You smarten up!' he yelled. 'You give good service.'

She sank back on the arm of the sofa, a hand to her reddened cheek with its sea blue nails. Her lipstick was half off her lips, the spray on her hair cloying. Mike was giving her too much of the hard stuff. He'd have to sort him out. She could earn hot money if she was clean. Not like this.

He took a twenty out of his pocket and flung it on the sofa. 'That's all you deserve.'

She went carefully for the note like a cowed dog.

Feliks' phone rang. He looked to see who was ringing, and put a severe finger to his lips to indicate Saffron should keep silent.

'Hello, my dear. How are things?' he said.

'I've sorted out the childminding for my daughter,' said Alison.

'That's wonderful,' said Feliks. 'So it's all clear for tonight. I'll meet you in the theatre bar at ten past seven. And we'll have an evening of culture.'

'I haven't been to the theatre in an age,' said Alison. 'I'm so looking forward to it.'

'The play has had a good review in the Sunday Times,' he said. 'The Theatre Royal is a charming theatre.'

They chatted for another few minutes. The conversation had quite changed his mood. It was all on course for tonight.

After ringing off, he screwed Saffron, and went back to work.

Chapter 26

Jack decided that he'd do one more hour cleaning out mortar, then have a blitz of mortaring. He'd lost time with the unexpected lovemaking, not at all regretted, and easily made up by working later. It'd been a beautiful surprise when she'd returned early. What began as an embrace became a scramble to the bedroom. He'd never got his coffee.

He'd remind her of it next time he saw her.

As he chipped on, he was aware of his inane grinning. As well he was up here, too self satisfied for ground level. And then, to top it all, she was coming over this evening, bringing food for them to cook together. No coffee, would he get dinner?

Would he care?

A man stumbled out of next door, doing up his trousers with one hand, clutching his jaw with the other. Was that blood? Saffron must pack a punch, he thought. Well, she was a big lady. The man had gone to a car, his head sank on the roof.

Was he ill or had he been bashed? Should he go down and help? He looked around for anyone else. Feliks wasn't about, the cement mixer silent.

The man had got in the car. Jack couldn't see him any longer as the car started. It jerked, stopped and started again. The man was in a hurry to get away, but not in the best of control. What had that been all about? One of Saffron's patrons. Money was usually the problem. That made him think of Feliks. He'd run a mile to save a penny. Was it too coincidental that he wasn't about? You're vulnerable when you visit a whore. No matter what happens, you're not likely to report it.

Not that he was tempted. His reply to Jean had been truthful. Prostitution was a dirty business. Too many penises in one place, with violent men cashing in. Sex slavery too. The women often in a bad way. Saffron last night had been desperate for something.

Don't judge, said Alcohol Halt. Easily said, harder to do. And sometimes, surely, you had to. A couple of whores came to Alcohol Halt. The women could be fierce in their judgements. Still on the game. Who would sleep with alcoholic junkies?

Enough men, they assured him.

The man had driven out of his sight. A lot of blood. Up here you saw too much. But Jean had caught him. He was stupidly grinning. In spite of thinking of prostitution and men beaten up, he was as soppy as a sunflower. Jean in his life. Difficult to believe what had blossomed in such a short time. They'd talked, she'd met Mia who had approved, seen a conjunction of two planets, and they'd made love. From tomorrow she would be working at his place.

It was overwhelming. He'd invited her to move in, and she hadn't rejected it. It was a revolution in his life.

The rain came quickly. He hadn't noticed the sky darkening, wrapped in his thoughts. And suddenly, out of nothing it seemed, the rain was belting down. He'd brought up his golf umbrella for such events, as there was no shelter up top. And these squalls could blow over quickly. He knelt low and sheltered under the umbrella, reluctant to go down straight away. There was blue in the sky; this could be a short squall.

Rainwater was rolling off the rooftop, turbulent in the gutter. He could hear it gurgling down the drainpipe. And he saw Jean leaving the house, a big umbrella over her. He only recognised her from her pale brown coat, as she scuttled along the road through darts of rain, until she was out of his view.

Busy woman. He could envisage that as a future problem. Sometime, a long way off, from the day he was living. She worked so hard, long hours, made oodles of cash. He'd have to book an appointment to make love. Or grab her between appointments, day or night. Or mid afternoon.

Was she thinking of him? Of course. She had to be. He could not believe it was just him so enraptured. She must be grinning too.

The rain slowed, and had all but stopped when the sun came out. There was a rainbow. Sublime from this height, arcing so wide, the colours full. It was double, one above the other. What a pity Jean had gone out. He would have liked to have shared it with her. Maybe she was seeing it from wherever she was. Though probably in thick traffic, seeing only the car in front.

He scoured the sky; the rain clouds had moved on. It was full sunlight again. He'd do the pointing before leaving. It was bad practice to leave brickwork unprotected.

He was down below, about to add water to his mortar, good job he'd covered the bucket, when it rained a second time. Jack decided that that was enough, bad practice or not. He'd pack up and leave early. The house wouldn't fall down. He'd do the pointing first thing in the morning.

Chapter 27

Mike and Lily came back from Stratford by the 25 bus. It was rush hour, not particularly noticeable coming back from Romford by train, as it was against the flow, but going from Stratford to Forest Gate by bus, he hit the crush. He had to fight to get on at the bus station, assisted by carrying Lily, as some allowed him preference, but more mobbed onto the bus with the selfishness of crowds, not caring he had a child in tow. He and Lily were packed in downstairs. He was holding her in his arms, and she grew heavier in the slow, packed bus. He would have liked to put her down but there was no room. As soon as he got home, he'd dump the kid on Jean, have a shower and head off to Mandy's. See what she'd taken.

The bus inched along, each stop a fighting queue battling with those trying to alight. He should have stayed another hour later at his mother's and avoided the rush hour, but she was persecuting him. Asking him about work, about Jean, why Lily wasn't talking yet. As if any of it was her business. He didn't need her advice, and so lied about himself and Jean. Their holiday plans and such rubbish. Then she was saying how early he and his sister had been talking. And was Lily normal? He wanted to hit her. This was exactly why he didn't go home very often. This inquisition. She made him feel like a six year old, every time.

At last Mike and Lily got off the bus. It had been raining, but they'd avoided it, luckily as he hadn't brought raincoats or an umbrella. Lily had been good. He shouldn't blame her, but he'd had her all day. Being so responsible, thinking in advance about toilets. He needed to dump her and be himself. He was an enforced parent. Fortunately there was a lot Lily didn't understand, notably about drugs and sex. Maybe being a late talker was no bad thing. She wasn't asking questions he didn't want to answer.

But he did want to unburden himself. Thrust the child into Jean's arms, and hotfoot away.

A thought struck him like a lightning bolt. He'd paid Feliks to kill Jean. But he wanted Jean to have custody. A day every few weeks would suit him. But with her dead, he'd be stuck with Lily. Every damned day. He shook himself; he wasn't thinking straight. His mother's diatribe and the rush hour had made him ratty. With Jean dead, he'd get the house. He'd get her money. Then he could take on an au pair, even a nanny. Someone shaggable maybe.

Carry on, Feliks.

At the house, he noted the builder had gone, the tower forlorn by the side of the house. What would he do with him when Jean croaked? Did the house really need re-pointing? Couldn't he just leave it as it was? Save the cash for more useful things.

Mike opened up, and looked in the sitting room. She wasn't there.

In the hallway, he called, 'Jean! We're home.'

No response. She might be working. He put Lily in the sitting room with her toys and ran upstairs to her office. The room was empty, her laptop was gone. She must still be at Maggie's. This was a downright liberty. He'd had Lily all day. He came downstairs.

'Are you hungry, Lily?'

She nodded. See, she understood. It was just that she didn't want to talk yet. He could understand that. It saved rows.

He wasn't particularly hungry himself, his mother overdid the cakes when they came round. Well, the visits weren't that frequent. Every couple of months. He gave Lily a banana and cream and made himself a coffee.

He'd resolved to keep his temper around Jean, but this was no joke. He had his own life to lead. He wasn't simply her childminder.

He phoned Mandy.

'Did you come round?' he asked.

'No,' she said. 'I thought about it. And decided it was too risky.'

'Too risky!' he exclaimed. 'There was no one here. Where was the risk?'

'I chickened out,' she said.

'So what are you going to do about money?'

She was silent for a second or two. 'Sell a few things. Go to a food bank. Try some auditions.'

'You hate them,' he retorted.

'Do I have any choice?'

He thought, I offered you the house on a plate, you had a choice there. He said, 'Come over now.'

'I've a bit of a headache,' she said. 'Come to my place.'

'Can't,' he said. 'I've got Lily till madam gets back.' He looked at the clock. 'She can't be long now. Soon as she is, I'll be over.'

'See you then.' She rang off.

Stupid woman. The whole house there for her taking, and she chickens out. You can only offer so much help. And then he recollected, he'd been offering Mandy *his* stuff. As it would be once Jean was off the scene. So just as well she hadn't come round. He had offered, she was the one who chickened out.

Where the hell was Jean? He phoned, and went straight to voicemail. She was probably drinking and feeding her face with that pal of hers. Maggie. He had no time for her. She didn't like him either. Stuck up cow.

Mike made himself some beans on toast, and ate them in the sitting room in front of the TV.

Chapter 28

Jack walked home. More convenient to leave the van near the house, instead of searching for a parking place on the road where he lived and another in the morning. All the materials and tools were either at the house or in the van. And it was only a short walk home.

Weird though, to walk. When working, he invariably drove. But with parking getting so difficult these days, you had to consider whether it was worth it. Or even driving anywhere, if it came to that, with the roads so jammed. But his van was his tool shed as well as his wagon, his shelter from the rain, his lunch room.

Not needed today. Mike had been out. There would be problems to come with him. It was hard keeping a love affair secret. With the two of them smiling inanely. You only need someone coming back early, the way Mike was caught yesterday with his trousers down.

What would he have done if Mike had marched in on them? Argue it out. Mike had his Mandy, he might say, so Jean had every right to do her thing. Not that Jean in the event would be passive. What a mighty row there'd be!

Could he still work there if it all came out? She was the paymaster, but Mike could be one hell of an obstacle to overcome, day after day. Especially if Jean were working at his place, and perhaps worse if she moved in. Little things could get problematic. Like using the toilet when he was working.

Or might Mike say – she's all yours, mate. Thank you for getting her out of my hair. Not likely. Jack had had his jealousies, thinking of one girlfriend he'd had enough of. Until she took a lover. It was then he'd felt the rejection, even though he no longer wanted her. Or only when he couldn't have her.

Best keep the affair secret for as long as possible. They might get away with it for the period he was working at the house. He'd have to talk it over with Jean. Work out a strategy.

He hoped she wouldn't have Lily tonight. So they could have the evening to themselves. Talk, make love, talk, learn about each other. Share the newness and excitement. A pity she'd missed the double rainbow. How would she like going out with the telescope? It wasn't essential. But it was his joy on a clear night to explore the heavens. She might regard it as a waste of her precious time. Such things had been said, not quite in those words, but previous girlfriends had rebelled.

But she had enjoyed the conjunction of Venus and Jupiter. So as long as it wasn't too cold, and if he was well prepared with a thermos, maybe a pizza... All to be found out.

He walked up the path to his front door. He'd have a shower and a snack, enough to stave off hunger, before the big meal. With any relationship you have to compromise. And that could be good. There would be things she wanted him to do with her. As well as vice versa.

Once in the main door, there was the door to the flat downstairs, and stairs going up to his. There was a third flat in the house, but that had a side door. He rarely saw the owner.

Jack went up his stairs and opened his front door. And at once heard the TV.

His plans were dashed.

Mia was laid out on the sofa, her schoolbag on the floor.

'What on earth are you doing here?' he exclaimed. 'You're supposed to be at Moira's tonight.'

'I didn't feel like going,' she said.

'Turn the TV off,' he said.

She did so. He sat down at the table. She sat up on the

sofa. She was growing up, her figure was filling out. This was a portent of complications to come. Three lives, a shifting Venn diagram of separation and coming together.

'I'm going out this evening,' he lied, knowing as soon as he said it that it was a stupid thing to say.

'I could still stay,' said Mia. 'I won't go out.'

'You can't,' he said.

She was silent a little while, her head drooped.

'Neither of you want me,' she said bitterly. 'Mum's out with her computer date. The perfect gentleman... And where are you going?'

'Actually, I'm not going out,' he conceded. 'Jean's coming here.'

'I could stay in the bedroom,' she said.

'Don't be silly.'

It had rocked him when she'd said 'Neither of you want me.' Two conflicting loves. Mia was here, and Jean was coming. If he wasn't so greedy for her... He must reassess. All it needed was for Jean to bring Lily – and it would be a repetition of last night. Was that so bad?

No. Simply that he'd been expecting so much more.

'Are you in love?' said Mia.

'Heading that way,' he admitted.

'I'm sorry,' she said. 'I've ruined your plans. But I'm not a chess piece. You can't just move me wherever you feel. I always feel in the way at Moira's.' She folded her arms. 'It's up to you. What do I do?'

'You can stay,' he said.

Yes, he could forcefully drive her to Moira's. No, he couldn't. He'd give up halfway; he hated seeing her miserable, so he might as well give up now.

'You can have the bedroom,' she said.

He laughed. She was growing up. 'Suppose Jean brings Lily?'

'I'll look after her.'

He considered that. He and Jean in the bedroom, Mia on the sofa, maybe with Lily. Might it work? It would subdue their lovemaking, the bedroom walls were thin. Maybe some slack time he could put in soundproofing. No solution for tonight though.

'We'll work it out,' he said. 'Jean said you were a charmer.'

'I should finish her book before she comes.'

'I'll make us a cup of tea.'

'No. I'll make it.' She rose. 'And thank you.'

'It was a shock seeing you here.' He laughed. 'So your mum's really excited, is she?'

'They're going to the Theatre Royal.' She headed for the kitchen, stopping at the door. 'She said, it was so nice to be going out with someone who wasn't after one thing.'

She went into the kitchen.

That cut him down to size. All men. All the time. The biological imperative. Were women that different? Jean hadn't seemed that different this afternoon. Maybe men were stirred more easily. Women, once stirred, caught up fast.

He and Mia had tea together. Mia made them cheese on toast, and talked about school, about Alison's date. Jack didn't say he knew him. That might get back to Alison, and he had little complimentary to say about Feliks. Let her learn.

Jack had a shower, Mia changed out of her school uniform. And did her homework without any goading.

Chapter 29

Jack phoned again, receiving the same recorded message from her voicemail. It was quarter to eight and Jean hadn't arrived, having been due at seven. Over the next twenty minutes he phoned four more times.

'I don't understand this,' said Jack. 'I saw her this afternoon. We confirmed the time. If something has come up, why hasn't she phoned?'

'Maybe she's lost her phone,' said Mia. She had done her homework and was reading Jean's book on Jack's laptop.

'Perhaps,' said Jack. He ceased marching up the sitting room, resting on the sofa arm. 'But if it was me, I'd still phone somehow or other. Borrow one, use a public phone.'

'Unless she's some place where she can't.' She'd stopped reading.

'Like where?'

Mia shrugged. 'I don't know.' Then added, as she struggled to think where, 'She could be busy working and she's forgotten the time. Maybe talking to people in the US. Different time zones.'

This had not occurred to Jack. Some crisis online? He had no idea what that could involve. But some panic in cyberspace – and everything else had gone from her head. Was that likely? He didn't know. It wasn't a world he occupied.

'She could be in hospital,' said Mia.

That reminded him of Trevor yesterday, searching for his mother. It was possible. She could be unconscious somewhere. On an operating table at this very moment. It was unlikely, but so was anything else. Even if Jean had changed her mind about their relationship, which he didn't believe, but then he didn't really know her, even if, surely she wouldn't be so cowardly as to not phone. Or at the very least come up with a lie. Say Lily was ill, or her grandmother was at death's door. A headache even.

At quarter past eight, he said, 'Let's go to her place.'

'You think she'll be there?'

'All I know is, she's not here. And I can't stand this waiting.' He removed his jacket from the hook by the door. 'Put your coat on.'

Jack phoned once more before they left, and went to the same voicemail.

He left a message: 'Please phone, Jean. I was expecting you well over an hour ago. If something has come up, please tell me.'

They left the flat. It was almost dark, the very end of twilight. The streetlights were on. There was a slight breeze, a bit of a chill in the air. They walked quickly.

'Will anyone be at her house if she isn't?' asked Mia.

'Her husband might be there,' he said. 'Maybe Lily too.'

'Does he know you're in love with his wife?'

Jack almost laughed at the formalism. 'No. She's getting a divorce. It'd be easier if they weren't living together; their marriage is broken. He's got a lady friend, so she feels she too can break the rules.'

'Might there be a fight between you and him?'

This hadn't occurred to Jack. It wasn't out of the question, if Mike guessed he and Jean's relationship.

'There won't be a fight,' he said, to reassure her. 'I'll make up some reason why I dropped round.'

They walked in silence for a while, both contemplating the coming encounter.

'We could say that I'd read her book and want to meet her,' said Mia.

'Good idea.' A sharp notion, he reflected, and Mia's presence softened things. Lovers don't bring their daughters round. 'That could work.'

'I've almost finished it. It's called *The Fifth Queen*. Just in case you need to know.'

She then told him the plot, but he stopped listening as she went on. Too confusing at the best of times, more so when thinking of Jean: what might have happened to her, whether she had changed her mind about their relationship, whether there was any point in calling round. He could only do so because she lived close by.

He didn't know what else to do.

Could he go to the police? Say her husband was dangerous. He dismissed the thought. She was barely ninety minutes late. He imagined the duty sergeant as Jack told him that Jean insisted she be at his place at seven. They must have a prepared line for such idiots.

It was ridiculous. He'd only met her yesterday. And only seen a fraction of her life. He was a fool to be going to her place.

They'd arrived at the house. The front curtains were drawn but the lights were on. Jack knew that to be the sitting room. Someone was in. Mike or Jean or both?

'That's my scaffolding tower,' he said, a delaying tactic, indicating the side of the house.

'You hired it, you mean.'

'Yes. It's not mine, clever clogs.' He took a deep breath. 'Okay, this is the line. We were just passing and you told me you wanted to meet Jean Lucas as you've just finished her book.'

'The Fifth Queen.'

'So keep a straight face. Pretend you're a fan.'

'I should've brought my autograph book.'

'Not if we are doing this on a whim.'

They climbed the steps to the front door. And Jack rang the bell. A long, double ring. His heart raced. Someone was in. But who would open up? Who did he want it to be? A shadow was showing on the glass.

The front door opened. It was Mike, in the same T-shirt he'd been wearing for two days. His face was sleepy, eyes two thirds shut.

'Jack!' he said, chirpy and upbeat. 'What are you doing here, pal?'

'This is my daughter,' said Jack nervously. 'We were passing...'

'I've just finished one of Jean Lucas' books,' joined in Mia, 'and I'd like to get her autograph.'

You haven't got your autograph book, remember, thought Jack.

'Sorry to disappoint you, but I'm afraid she's not here,' said Mike. 'She should have been back ages ago. Why don't you come in? I could do with some company.' He opened the door wide for them. 'Do you live nearby?'

'Earlham Grove,' said Mia.

'No distance,' said Mike as they came in.

They came into the hallway. Jack saw the child gate at the top of the stairs was closed. Lily must be in bed. And so she should be, this time of night. Mike ushered them in the sitting room. The large flat screen TV was on. Doctors and nurses were rushing down a corridor with a man on a trolley. Mike switched it off with the remote.

Jack sat on the sofa, Mia took an armchair.

'Do you want a drink, Jack? Sorry I don't know your name...'

'I'm Mia.'

Jack said, 'Have you a coke or something?'

'On the wagon, mate?'

Jack nodded. 'I smashed a car up under the influence. Just about walked out alive. So that's it for me.'

'I could offer you some weed...' He indicated Mia.

'No good,' said Jack with a shake of the head. 'It only makes me want to drink.'

'Coke then. I'll see what we've got in the fridge.'

Mike left them.

Mia waited a few seconds, then said quietly, 'She's not here.'

Jack nodded. 'Yeh. But we have to stay a little while. Good manners.'

Up in a corner of the room, there was a video screen showing a black and white image of a child in bed. Clearly Lily. She turned over in bed and burbled. The modern way to keep an eye on a child in a big house. Jean would have a screen in her office too, he thought. He hadn't noticed one in the bedroom, but then he hadn't looked on the only occasion he'd been there.

So Mike didn't know where Jean was. There was no sign he was pretending, he'd even invited them in. Jack wanted to leave now. Why stay? Except having come in and accepted a drink, the rules said you must stay longer.

'It's a big house for just three of them,' said Mia.

'She's got an office upstairs,' said Jack. 'One of the bedrooms. Four in all up top. There's another for his music.' He added quietly, 'he doesn't use it much.'

Mike returned with two glasses of coke and ice. He was rocking slightly on his feet as if on board a ship. Half stoned, thought Jack. At least it had mellowed him.

He gave them both a coke.

'Do you mind if I have a whisky, Jack?'

'Your house,' said Jack, taking a sip. He'd have to finish the drink now before they could leave. What on earth were they to talk about?

'It won't be mine when Jean's finished with me,' said Mike with a grin. He'd gone to the cocktail cabinet and pulled down the lid. 'I told you we were divorcing, didn't I?'

'You did,' said Jack, though not sure which of the couple had informed him.

Mike poured himself a generous tot of Famous Grouse. 'She'll end up with this place. I'll end up on the street.'

'I'm sorry,' said Jack, as Mike crossed the room to sit down on the long sofa.

'Not as sorry as I am, mate,' said Mike with a broad grin. He took a drink. 'You were here yesterday. You know what happened. She caught me with Mandy.' He shrugged. 'She must've guessed something was going on. Well, it had been long enough. So she came back early to catch us at it. Quite a scene.' He turned to Mia. 'Sorry if I am shocking you, young lady.'

She said cautiously, 'Lots of people get divorced these days.'

'She should be here,' exclaimed Mike. 'Hours ago. She went off to see her writer friend Maggie this afternoon. And she hasn't come back.'

Jack didn't correct him. She hadn't gone to Maggie's, he knew, and she had come back. Then gone out again. Information he didn't wish to divulge as he might be asked how he knew.

'I haven't Maggie's number,' said Mike. 'Never needed it. I looked in her office for it earlier, but couldn't find it. Address lists are all electronic these days.'

'Just tell her I came round,' said Mia. 'And I really liked *The Fifth Queen*.'

'Never read it,' said Mike dryly. 'Never read any of her books. And I can't imagine I will now. She started writing when she was pregnant with Lily. And I can't believe how quickly she's taken off. An internet success. I would be quite proud of her, if I didn't dislike her so much.' He grinned broadly. 'I'm stuck looking after Lily,' he went on, 'until she gets back. I want to go off and see Mandy. My girlfriend,' he added for Mia's benefit. 'She shouldn't do this to me,' he exclaimed angrily, hammering a fist on the low table and making the glasses jump. 'We should be civilised, while we go through this painful process. The fucking cow.' He held up his hands pacifyingly. 'Sorry, sorry. That was out of order. But I detest being used like this.'

Jack couldn't think of what to say. He'd wanted to ask Mike where else Jean might be, but that obviously wasn't appropriate. Mike didn't care and might ask why Jack wanted to know.

Mia said, 'I like Lily.'

Wrong, wrong, thought Jack in panic. The child is supposed to be a stranger. You have never met mother or daughter before – that is the line. Mike was looking puzzled, peering at Mia closely. This could all blow up.

'How have you met Lily?' said Mike.

'I haven't,' said Mia. 'There's pictures of her on your wife's Facebook page. She's a pretty little girl.'

'I suppose so,' said Mike with a shrug. 'She gets less pretty when you've been stuck with her all day.'

Jack was relieved at Mia's quick thinking. Had they stayed long enough? Mike continued staring at Mia, who was looking at an abstract painting across the room.

The doorbell rang.

'I am popular this evening,' exclaimed Mike rising. 'All go at the Lucas house. Where it's all happening.' He left the room.

Mia waited until he was safely gone.

'Sorry,' she hissed. 'Nearly blew it.'

'You gave me a heart attack.'

He wondered who might be at the door and listened out. It could be Jean, lost her keys along with her phone. The police to report an accident. He could hear a mumble of conversation. It wasn't Jean then. She'd come straight in. And likely the conversation would be a lot louder.

'Have we stayed long enough?' said Mia behind her hand.

'We have,' said Jack. 'Finish your coke.'

She drank the remnant in the glass. Jack and Mia rose and started towards the door of the room, only to meet Mike and Saffron coming in. She was in her short house coat, bare feet, hair awry.

'Hello,' said Jack awkwardly.

'Hello,' said Saffron, blinking rapidly. He guessed she hadn't recognised him.

'We have to go,' said Jack to Mike.

'I've homework to finish,' said Mia. 'Thanks for the coke.'

'Nice to have met you.' He slapped Jack's hand. 'See you tomorrow, mate.'

Jack and Mia left.

Chapter 30

Mike and Saffron were on the patio, at the table. He'd been tempted to smoke in the sitting room, but had never done it before. Jean would scream and rage if she smelt the faintest whiff inside. So he'd put on his coat and gone outside. Saffron was shivering but not enough to complain.

She took a draw of the glass crack-pipe, her eyes lighting up. She was rapidly soothed and breathed freely.

'This is good stuff,' she oozed. 'Better than yesterday's crap. All filler and no buzz.'

'I had a go at my supplier,' said Mike. 'Told him I had other options if he couldn't give quality.' He took the pipe from her. There was little smoke left, the lady had quite a suck. Not surprising with that chest. Maybe later he'd take relief. In the meantime, smoke. Fill. He held the lighter under the enclosed bowl and flicked it into flame. The residue boiled and smoke filled the chamber.

Mike took it down, deep into his lungs. The world became milder, kinder to him. He was important, he mattered. Without him, nothing could happen anywhere.

She said, 'That Feliks is one dangerous guy.'

He smiled broadly. He wanted him to be.

'That old lady,' she said, her head back, looking into the clouds. 'The one they are all looking for. He was screaming at her. I had a punter on the go. He wanted to know what was going on. I said it was S&M... And then she's not around anymore. What do you make of that?'

Mike took another drag. His face was set in a grin; it had no other mode.

'That she doesn't like being screamed at. She vamoosed.'

Saffron watched the pipe, the smoke diminishing inside,

'Today, he smacked up a punter. Broke his jaw maybe. Didn't need to do that. A warning maybe. A threat. But he smashed him round the face with his club. He was spitting teeth.'

'He's a killer,' murmured Mike.

'I don't want someone so violent,' said Saffron, biting her lower lip. 'He keeps putting my rent up. Thinks I'll pay anything just to stay in those rooms.'

'He gives you protection,' said Mike taking another puff. The world was his dream. If only he had his guitar. It was always in the wrong place. Too far upstairs, another hemisphere. Here was the place. He passed her the pipe. The universe was made for sharing.

'The word gets out I got a pimp like that, I'll have no punters.'

She sucked deeply. He put his hand on her thigh. It was firm, thick and vibrant. The pulse of the cosmos.

'You want it, you pay,' she said thickly, the gas entering her bloodstream.

'I am paying,' he said, indicating the pipe with a broad grin.

'Make up a new blow,' she said, 'then you can shoot your dick.'

Chapter 31

Jack and Mia were home again. After leaving Mike's they'd gone down to Woodgrange High Street to pick up chicken and chips. Seated at the table, they emptied the boxes onto plates.

'Makes it seem like a home cooked meal,' said Jack.

'Mum never lets me eat this stuff.'

'I wouldn't normally,' said Jack, 'it's just that with what's been happening...'

He didn't say anymore, as he wasn't sure what had happened. They simply knew a place where Jean wasn't. That left the rest of the world where she might be.

'Mike didn't seem so bad,' said Mia. She was eating a chicken breast with her fingers, mouth and chin greasy.

Jack thought if Mike'd had any idea why they had really come, then she'd have seen a different side of him. They wouldn't have got coke. There might have been blood. He was poking chips in his mouth. Although they had cutlery, it lay unused on the table.

'He didn't suspect,' he said.

'Why should he?' she said. 'We stuck to our story.'

Jack laughed. 'If your mum only knew what I involved you in.'

As he picked at a chicken wing, he felt some guilt. He was having an affair with a married woman. A woman going for a divorce, which perhaps mitigated the charge. But they'd been in the sitting room of the husband, lying to him, he and his thirteen year old daughter.

Alison would kick him to Timbuktu if she ever found out.

'I'm glad you're here,' he said.

'But you'd rather she was.' She was eating a drumstick with both hands.

He shrugged. 'It's different,' he said. 'With adults. You know what you are to me. Don't forget that.' He didn't like saying words like love. They sounded cheap, like in a crap film, besides his having said them at times when he didn't mean it. A debased currency.

He was glad she was here; that was sincere. He had a responsibility tonight. Earlier he'd felt desperate, waiting for Jean. So desperate, he'd even gone to see her husband. His daughter's presence meant that he'd come home again. Suppose she hadn't been here? He would have still gone round to Mike's. Then what? Gone where afterwards?

He wasn't the best of parents. Not the worst either. There were those that sacrificed their lives for their kids. Lived, it seemed, just for them, every house move, every job change, putting the kids first. While Alison had offloaded Mia on to Moira, or so she thought, while she got on with her love life. His own intention too. Except it hadn't happened.

It could have been a disastrous night. A fight with Mike, a visit to the pub, and not KFC. The parent in him held on tight.

They cleared up and had tea.

Jack said, 'Wash, clean your teeth and bed.'

'Can I read the end of Jean's book in bed?'

'How much more have you got?'

'About three chapters.'

He agreed, and she went off to wash. He picked up the phone. What was the point? He'd rung about ten times that evening. She had enough messages to fill a bottle twice over. He put down the phone.

Why was night harder to deal with than day? No work, less light. The streets shadowy, with all your fears under the trees.

Chapter 32

Mike had had his roll with Saffron. On the sofa as well. Up yours, Jean. He was too stoned to care if his wife caught them. Not that they were long. It didn't matter. He was immortal.

Or had been. He was getting more mortal as the drug wore off. He would die some time or other. Maybe in a thousand years.

He liked the purity of Saffron. She didn't care whether he came or not. A transaction. Sex for drugs. She was pretty groggy anyway, more asleep than awake. Though he could talk, it was that third blow that killed his cock.

A pity Jean hadn't caught them at it. It would show what he thought of her. That he could bring a whore in and have her on the sofa. Anything he liked now that divorce was happening. And Feliks had the solution.

She must have a lover somewhere. That Maggie. A regular session. That would fit. A couple of lesbians. Humping in the hay while he looked after Lily. The quicker Feliks did his business the better.

And that builder coming round. It was odd. If he hadn't had his daughter with him, he might have thought he was after Jean. Hoping Mike wasn't in. Would Jean be interested in that boring fart? Doesn't drink, doesn't want a blow. Could he even do it?

Mike considered; he could sleep down here or he could go upstairs. Upstairs, yeh. And maybe he should clean up his gear. Shouldn't he? Do it in the morning. The smash was safe in the poly bag even if it rained. Who'd nick it out on the patio?

Mike shut the French windows, and turned the key in the lock.

Satisfied, Jean?

Not until she'd got him out of here. Then, and only then, would the cow be satisfied. He staggered to the door, switched off the light, and made his way up the stairs, rocking from banister to wall. He sat down on a step halfway up. Tomorrow, he'd talk to Feliks, order him to get a move on. Or he wanted his money back.

He'd lay it down. Chapter and verse. Give him a deadline.

He went up another three steps and sat down again. There was no hurry; this was his house. No one was going to tell him what to do in it. He'd shag whoever he wanted to, in the bedroom, on the sofa. A pliable nanny would be a good investment. Or was that just another name for a wife? Except you could sack a nanny. A wife could make you homeless.

He liked that. He should write it down. Smash made him witty.

He moved up another two steps on his arse. He should move his guitar and keyboard to the sitting room. Then he would play them. Being all the way up here, they were out of the way. Too far to go. His music should be on tap. Like sex and drugs.

He was a pleasure machine. On Earth to be pleasured and give pleasure. What else was life for?

He'd reached the top, and had trouble with the child gate. Why was the latch so complicated? In the end, he climbed over, and staggered on the hall carpet to the bedroom.

It didn't matter how long it took. Time was relative anyway. And this was his house. He'd paid good money, he'd suffered for it, he told the bedroom door.

He opened it and switched on the light. Jean was naked on the bed with her skull broken.

PART THREE:
THE ROAD TO BECKTON

Chapter 33

Mike washed his face. Over and over. He cleaned his teeth. He washed his face again. The thing about smash was that you saw things, things that weren't there. Sort of waking dreams. He'd had it before. You saw something you wanted, but maybe in a form you didn't like.

He soaked his hair, washed his face again. Then sat on the edge of the bath and wiped himself on the towel, daring himself to go back into the bedroom.

He'd only seen her for an instant. Like a film. Or more like, what did they call it? A hologram. 3D. Then he flicked the light off. Amazing what the mind can make up. But then it makes the world, every second of the day, makes words, makes music. A dead wife is child's play.

A dream of a dead wife, he meant. Not a real one. At least, not here. To be sure, he'd been thinking of the time when she was dead. When she was off his back, and he had the house and his freedom. When he could screw who he wanted wherever he wanted. And the desire made the dream.

Didn't it?

He went back out into the hall and saw Lily in her Winnie the Pooh pyjamas walking towards him. She was rubbing her eyes. His daughter was real, he was sure. He went up to her, picked her up. Weighty enough. You couldn't dream weight, could you?

He couldn't think far ahead. Or do more than one thing. He had a daughter awake in the night. He had a wife, either out somewhere with her lesbian lover or in the bedroom. Out would be simpler. Lots simpler. He didn't like the dream he'd had. A nightmare really. It left too many things for him to consider.

He put down Lily. She was clinging to his leg. He had to find out about Jean. Whether she was a figment or whether she was in the bedroom as he dreamed. But he had Lily. He knew if he took Lily back to bed in this state she would insist he stayed with her. Sometimes she crept into their bed in the early hours.

He would just look in, hold Lily out of the way, just in case. Taking her hand, he walked to the bedroom door. He opened the door, just wide enough to get his head and arm round.

Mike switched on the light.

Jean was there, as he'd seen her before. Lying on her back, naked, a great gash in her crown, blood over her face. Exactly as he'd seen her before. She was real.

The door pushed a little. He wasn't sure what was happening for a second. And then saw Lily in the room. She was at her mother's head, her hands rubbing her mother's face.

Mike was at once in. He lifted his daughter and took her out of the room. Along the corridor and to the bathroom. There, he washed her hands; there was blood on her pyjamas. He'd see to that later. He locked the bathroom door.

The pig had done it. And left her here for him to see. Well, he'd seen her. That wasn't the point at all. Not what he'd paid for.

He took out his phone, and phoned Feliks. A female recording told him that Feliks wasn't answering his phone at the moment, and he should phone back later. He tried three more times, and the stupid lady told him the same thing.

He took Lily downstairs. In the sitting room, he took some of her soft toys out of the playbox and laid them on the carpet.

'I'll be back in a minute,' he said.

She ran after him. He pushed her back into the room and

she started crying. He closed the sitting room door on her, and was quickly out the front door and along to next door.

He rang Feliks' bell. He rang it on and on. His finger on the buzzer, pressing continuously. The bastard had dropped him in it. He continued ringing.

The door was opening. A dishevelled Saffron came to the door. She stared at him, half asleep.

'I need Feliks,' he said.

'He's gone out,' she said wearily. 'All dressed up. I haven't heard him come back. Go away. It's late.'

'I need him.'

'He's not here.'

And she closed the door on him. He stood at the door, not knowing what to do. Then turned and walked slowly back. On the pavement, he saw Lily, barefoot in her pyjamas, crying.

Mike picked her up and went back into the house.

On the carpet, he played with her. With Snaky, Ellie the Elephant and Ringy the ringtailed lemur. They were good friends, but sometimes they fought. Now they were building a house out of bricks.

He phoned Mandy. It took her some time to answer.

'Are you coming over?' she said drowsily.

'I've got an emergency here,' he said.

'What sort of emergency?'

He told her about the body in the bedroom, and that Feliks wasn't at home.

'Does he mean you to phone the police?' she said.

'I can't do that,' he exclaimed. 'They'll think I did it.'

She was silent a while. And then said, 'I'll be over.'

She rang off. Good old Mandy. Someone he could rely on, at least. She would know what to do. He should make some coffee. He needed to think straight, get the fog out of his head. Lily was playing with her animals, happily enough. She had blood on the sleeves of her pyjamas.

He left her and went into the kitchen where he put the kettle on. He needed a jug full of coffee. A little later, Lily came and joined him. He gave her yogurt in a bowl and had one himself. The kettle boiled and switched off. Such ordinary things. He shovelled half a dozen spoonfuls of coffee grounds into the cafetiere and filled it to the brim.

He was drinking his second cup when he heard Mandy arrive. She had a key. He ran out into the hallway to greet her. She had brought her bike in and was laying it against the wall. Once secure, she came to him. And they embraced.

After a minute, they disentangled and went into the kitchen. Lily was at the table, rubbing her eyes sleepily.

'Have a coffee,' said Mike. 'I'll take Lily to bed.'

He picked the child up, half over his shoulder, and left the room. Still a little shaky, he climbed the stairs. The child gate was open from when he'd come down. Up and down too many times. He tried to ignore the main bedroom as he carried Lily to hers. She didn't resist when he put her to bed, her eyes drooping. He really should change those pyjamas. Except there were more pressing things to do.

He stayed for a few minutes as she drifted into sleep. Then went back down to the kitchen where Mandy sat with her coffee. She was wearing a long sleeved, green hoodie top, the sleeves rolled up for her cycle over, her hair tied back in an efficient ponytail.

She said, 'You have two choices. Either call the police or get rid of the body.'

This statement of the obvious threw him. Each choice fraught with risk.

'The police will think I did it,' he exclaimed. 'She was going for a divorce. She probably told her Facebook group that she found us in bed...' He stopped. 'No cops. I've already got a record for dealing.'

'Then we have to dump the body,' said Mandy, 'some place it won't be found in a hurry. Then we'll have time for a clean up before you need to report her missing.'

'How?' he said. 'Where?' Relieved she was thinking for him. He was still fogged.

'We have to get her into the car. Have you got her car keys?'

'Yes. She didn't take them off me. Only a matter of time.' He half grinned, at once shutting it down. 'Where do we take her? Epping Forest?'

'We could,' admitted Mandy. 'That's a bit of a trek. And we'd have to bury her. But I was thinking of the beach near the Woolwich Ferry. I used to go there picking up flotsam for an art class. There's a deep muddy area. Bikes disappear in it.'

'She's naked,' he exclaimed. 'She'll float.'

Mandy thought a while, then said, 'We put her in a coat. Fill the pockets with stones...'

His head dropped into his hands. 'Oh, this is awful. Why did I give him the money?'

'He's a prick,' she said. 'Not to be trusted.'

'You'd've done a better job,' he said.

She shrugged. 'We can't sit here drinking coffee. You bring the car round. I'll find some clothes for her.'

Chapter 34

Mike walked up Clova Road, scouring both sides of the street. He'd only met one other person, and he was staggering drunk, seeing very little in his effort to keep upright. Most lights were off in the houses, the Victorian facades forbidding in the shadows. The wind had picked up, and the leaves on the street trees flickered in the street lights, throwing phantoms on to the pavement and the parked cars. No stars were out in the dense, dark sky. Coming out without a coat, Mike, at any other time, would have felt the chill, but anxiety made him oblivious.

Had he missed her car? A silver Audi, not a remarkable car, much like many others. Jean was always complaining about the difficulty of parking here, and sometimes had to park on one of the side roads.

Which one? That's if he hadn't missed it on Clova Road.

All the time, he was still in disbelief, Jean had been up in the bedroom. Dead. Since he'd come back with Lily from his mother's, she'd been lying there, her head smashed in. He'd gone upstairs to put Lily to bed, and then again to find Maggie's phone number in Jean's office, but had not gone into the bedroom. He'd smoked himself soppy and only then thought of shuteye. All that while she'd been there. Waiting for him.

A sort of revenge.

Feliks had had a clear afternoon to do it. No one in the house. All he had to do was evade the builder. And get it done. Well, he had. But what a mess he'd left! Leaving Mike to tidy up while he went out on the razzle with one of his conquests. Was that because he hadn't paid him enough? He'd wanted five thousand, but he only had three thousand seven hundred... If he paid him the balance would he get rid of her?

Except he wasn't around. He had deliberately gone out and left Mike to pick up the pieces. How naïve of him to trust the man. Feliks had done the minimum, and left him with a corpse, like a cat bringing in a dead bird for inspection. His to clear away.

He found the car a little way down Norwich Road, and hoped it had enough fuel to get them to the Woolwich Ferry. He climbed in and switched on the engine. Half a tank. Good. Jean was efficient at such things, it was he who let the tank run down to almost empty. To her annoyance.

Not any longer.

Mike drove back to Clova Road. Now, where to park? He couldn't see a space near the house, which, of course, was why he'd had to go so far to find the vehicle. In the end, he parked across a driveway about forty metres up. No one was likely to come out, this early in the morning.

He walked back to the house, and found Mandy waiting on the step. She was wearing rubber household gloves. Mandy was smart, she was thinking.

'Where have you been?' she said.

'Couldn't find the car,' he said. 'I walked up and down the road, and then found it on Norwich. As it is, I had to park up the road.'

She gave him a hug. He embraced her, welcoming her warmth, and would have stayed forever, but she stepped away.

'Work to do.'

He nodded. 'The sooner this is done the better.'

'We need to carry her down to the hallway,' she said. 'Then you can bring the car along.'

They went upstairs. He cursed Feliks, again and again, for putting him through this pain. What would he do without Mandy here? He couldn't handle the body himself.

He'd have to cut her up and get rid of her piecemeal. How, with Lily around?

In the upstairs hallway, she gave him a pair of gloves.

'Keep our prints off the body.'

'Of course.' He put them on gratefully.

In the bedroom, on the bed, Jean was dressed in an orange tracksuit, her bare feet a pallid blue. Over her head was a black plastic bag, tied tightly at the neck.

'To keep blood off us,' said Mandy.

Jean wasn't heavy, so they had little trouble getting her out into the upstairs hallway. Going downstairs was trickier, but with a few breaks, they got to the bottom. There, they took a breather, the body lying face up on the carpet, arms by her body, legs straight out as if Jean was assisting them by making no fuss. The black bag over her head gave her the appearance of a mannequin put aside after the display.

Mandy kneeled down by the body.

'So quiet, aren't you?' she said. And slapped her round the face. 'That's for pulling my hair, bitch.' She slapped the other cheek. 'That's for twisting my nose!'

'Leave her,' exclaimed Mike. 'Have some respect.'

'A little late for that.' She rose slowly, looking down at the corpse in disdain. She pushed the head with her foot. 'You can screw her if you want. She won't object now.'

'I just want her out of the house. Away! Anywhere.'

'You don't want a threesome?'

'Stop it, Mandy. I can't take this.'

She put a rubber gloved hand on his shoulder. 'Get a grip, Mike. This is the easy bit. No one's watching us in the hall.'

'Just don't slap or kick her,' he said. 'Please.' There were tears welling.

'OK. No fun.' She bit her lip. 'We need to get the car outside, so we can get her in the boot in one heave.'

'If anyone sees us... we're goners.'

'There's no one about, Mike,' she snapped. 'Shape up.'

Mandy opened the front door and went down the path. A few seconds later, she came back.

'If we lay her right against the front wall, she'll be out of sight. And pretty close to the road, for a quick heave ho.'

They took an end each and carried her out of the house, down the steps, to the lee of the low garden wall. In the shadow, she could only be seen by someone coming up their path. Mike headed off to get the car. Mandy closed the front door, and sat on the bottom step, waiting. She looked at the houses opposite. Mostly in darkness, a few lights on in hallways. No traffic, this was a quiet, residential road, tree-lined and respectable.

Mike drove to the middle of the road, just outside the house. He left the vehicle there, the engine still running. They carried the body out, across the pavement and between the cars, dropping the corpse in the boot, folding the legs to get her completely in. And slamming the door shut.

They leaned on each other, partly from tiredness, partly relief at having the body out of the house and out of sight. It might be late, but a couple hugging by a car was not suspicious. They could be lovers parting or seizing the moment.

'There's a car coming,' said Mike, indicating headlights some way off. 'Let's get on the move.'

They got into the car, he taking the driving seat, she the passenger, and drove off. It was only when he was turning off their road, that he remembered that they'd left Lily.

Chapter 35

The black BMW stopped in the middle of the road, outside Feliks' house. In the front were a man and a woman in black clothing. In Russian, the man told her to go now, to be quick but no mistakes. She nodded her assent, adjusting her industrial rubber gloves. Taking the can, funnel and length of rope, she climbed out of the car.

Without hesitating, she strode up the path, taking the few front steps at the double. The woman opened the letterbox in the front door and inserted the funnel end. She unscrewed the lid of the can and began pouring the liquid in, taking care not to spill any down the door front. A little that did, she wiped away with a tissue. She let the liquid drip out of the funnel, before pouring in more, not rushing in order to keep the noise down and avoid spillage.

And then, the can was empty, the contents puddled on junk mail and the rug by the foot of the door. She screwed back the lid and gave the thumbs up to the driver, who was watching from the car. He returned the gesture, meaning the road was still clear. She pushed the prepared rope through the letterbox, advancing it further and further in, until only a few inches were showing.

Taking a lighter from her pocket, shielding it with her body, she flicked it into flame. The woman touched the fire to the rope taper. The end sizzled and went out. Taking the tissue out of her pocket, she wiped the end of the rope with the fluid. And then held the flame again, longer this time, her gloved fingers almost catching. The rope end glowed to bright red and, in a hissing eagerness, the fire leapt along the length.

She rapidly gathered up the can and funnel, and ran to the safety of the car. There was a sudden whoosh behind her. She turned to see an orange flame flaring behind the glass of the door.

The car door was open, the driver was hissing for her to get in. She got in the passenger side, and as she was slamming the door, the BMW drove off.

Ten minutes later, a woman, in bed in the next door house, smelt acrid smoke through her open window. She rose, went to the window, opened it further and put her head out. And saw the house next door ablaze.

The fire brigade were there in five minutes. Utterly drilled, the team broke down the front door and were hosing water into the hallway shortly afterwards. A fire fighter smashed Saffron's front window and a second hose was directed in.

It wasn't long before the fire was out, leaving the house full of black smoke. Three yellow helmeted fire fighters in breathing apparatus went in. They smashed down the remnants of Saffron's door, which had burnt through, and searched the smoke filled rooms. A further three went up the stairs to Feliks' flat, and others down the outside stairs to the basement, breaking their way in.

Over the shoulder of a fire fighter, Saffron, unconscious, was carried out, and immediately put in a waiting ambulance. Her hair was frizzled, her nightdress black with soot, but she was breathing, albeit somewhat croakily. Paramedics gave her oxygen as they drove off, siren blaring.

No one was found in the top flat or in the basement.

Chapter 36

Mike was driving down Green Street. Brightly lit, even this time of night. Sleek mannequins in saris shone in the bright windows of the closed shops. Though not every sales outlet was closed. A few short-skirted prostitutes maintained their stations, awaiting custom. A black cab passed the other way, its display showing it was available for hire. A blue car cruised the other side, a punter weighing up the wares. They caught up with a burly black man jogging, in a green track suit and red woolly hat, a boxing club stencilled on his back.

'Should we be stopped, for any reason,' said Mike, his fingers rapping on the steering wheel, 'what do I say? Not that I want to be. Believe me, I don't. Not with this cargo.'

'Say you're driving home,' she said.

'We're going the wrong way,' he exclaimed.

They were silent a few seconds, considering narratives.

'You couldn't sleep,' she suggested, 'so you're out for a drive.'

'So why are you with me?'

She thought a moment. 'I'll hide. Get out, if I can.'

He wasn't sure he liked that. Being left by himself to cope. But he could see the sense of it. The story was he couldn't sleep, so was driving around by himself. You wouldn't drag a girlfriend along. He'd say, he often did it. Yes, he reflected, better Mandy was out of the picture. He was more likely to be believed on his own. If he could hold his nerve.

They were passing the old West Ham stadium. It was planned to be a shopping centre and housing, that sort of thing. On some other occasion, he might have pointed it out to Mandy, the mock turrets, and talked about football matches he'd been to. How rubbish they were this season.

All meaningless.

They crossed the Barking Road, with its statue of West Ham's World Cup heroes. The four from 1966, Bobby Moore and Martin Peters. Who were the others? He should know. Was Nobby Stiles a West Ham player? Or was he confusing him with someone else? More than twenty years before he was born, all that. Those grainy, black and white pictures. They were a long way from the glory days.

Miles and miles.

He headed down Central Park Road, a bit vague on this area. When they'd set off he'd wanted to put on the satnav, but she'd said no. It would tell anyone where they were going. All you need do is keep driving, she'd said, you are bound to hit the river. All very well for her to say, she wasn't at the wheel. You only have to go down a few back streets and you don't know whether you are heading north, south, east or west.

He felt so conspicuous on these night time streets. Respectable people tucked up in bed. Burglars climbing garden walls, whores strutting the pavement, clubbers coming home by cab, bug-eyed with poppers. Murderers with a body in the boot.

He stopped the car, looking around wildly. 'I don't know where we are.'

'Straight on, and you'll get to High Street South,' she said.

'You sure?'

'Yes. I've cycled this way.'

'Why don't you drive?'

'No,' she said. 'You're the driver. If anyone stops us, I hide or get out. It's you that's got to face them.'

He drove on, not too happy, while she navigated: straight on then a right turn on to High Street South. Keep going, she told him, and you get to the Newham Way. Across it and you are on the road to the Woolwich Ferry.

The police siren came out of nowhere. Mike jerked in alarm and saw in his rear view mirror a car some way behind them, top light circling.

'Who's he after?' he exclaimed.

'You,' she said. 'You're not exactly driving straight.'

'Bollocks, bollocks, bollocks!' He hit the steering wheel with both fists, and then put his foot on the gas. 'The old bill are not catching me.'

She was looking behind.

'He's speeding up,' she said.

They came to the Newham Way just after the lights changed. They shot across, through a red light, as a car hooted and braked into a skid. And they were over. Mandy, all the while, watching the whirling light.

'He's across,' she exclaimed.

'Bastard!'

This was a race, having started, he had to win. Maybe if he'd stopped back there, he could have talked his way out of erratic driving, perhaps swapped seats with Mandy before he was breathalysed. But the stuff he smoked didn't show up on breathalysers. Didn't they ask you to walk a straight line? Too late for all that. The cop knew they had something to hide and would search the car.

They were flying down Woolwich Manor Way, taking the centre of the road, their headlights breaking the dark. Just as well, there was no other traffic.

'There's another cop's car!' she yelled. 'Get off the main road or they'll cut you off!'

Mike took the next side road, Tollgate Road, his foot hard down as soon as he cleared the corner. She was watching the two flashing lights in pursuit, knowing they must be radioing ahead. She put her hands over her ears, the sirens were as piercing as bee stings. A car was coming their way, no doubt wondering what the fuss was. Mike zig-zagged round it and shot on.

'There's a helicopter!' exclaimed Mandy. She could see it above, light flashing, heading their way.

They've got us, she thought. Chased from behind, watched from up top, all the cops need is a car waiting ahead. And it must be already on its way.

'Off this road,' she yelled. 'It's our only chance.'

Mike made a sudden turn into a side street. Too fast. The car was skidding, the steering wheel useless, control lost, twisting and spinning, banging like insects in a box, victims of what they hit. First a parked car, bouncing off to the other side of the road, hitting another, then knocked across the road to strike a third. And finally halting. Their speed defused in the impacts.

Mandy was shaken, but not hurt, and undid her seatbelt. She was still wearing her household gloves as if she were about to wash the sink. Mike was slumped forward, the balloon bag engulfing him like a monster amoeba. In the second or so of careening, she was total adrenaline. They were coming; she must flee.

She opened the door the tiniest amount and rolled out, closing it behind her. The last car they'd hit was a high-wheeled four by four. She rolled under it, hearing the chopper circling overhead. The sirens of the chasing cars were growing louder. One stopped, its blue light splashing the houses and road. Mandy slipped out from under the car, into a few feet of clear space and under a white van.

The other police car had arrived. Mandy stayed still, laying flat on the road. She might evade the coppers on foot but the chopper would spot her if she wasn't careful. She'd seen chases on TV, the fierce light from a helicopter picking out the fugitives on the ground. She would have to wait, and hope she could get away.

There was little she could see from her refuge. Patterns of circling light on the roadway, from the cars and helicopter above; the cops would be round the crashed car.

167

The throb of the helicopter went through her, there were urgent cries. She thought Mike was probably OK. Of course, he'd be caught with the body in the boot. There'd be no doubt they'd search the car. All she could hope for was that he wouldn't drag her in.

She had to get away and clean up.

The helicopter was leaving. The pounding of the engine eased away. New crooks to hunt down. Better for her, with only those on foot around, and the attention on Mike and the car. She figured the optimum time for a getaway was when they opened the boot. That would hold their attention, oh, it would! while she made her getaway, staying in the shadows, out of their ken, while they phoned and jabbered.

She lay still, trying to breathe easily. Waiting. Boots came rapidly past her. There was shouting up ahead. Car doors slammed. She couldn't make sense of what was happening where. How many cops' cars were there? What were they doing? Was Mike OK? Did he need medical help?

Then she heard someone yell, 'Over here! Look at this!'

And knew they'd opened the car boot. She heard people running, expletives, saw boots going in one direction. Mandy rolled out, between cars. She crawled on to the pavement, lifting herself into a low run, heading away from the commotion, down the road as fast as she dared. And diving into a house gateway. She stayed still behind the garden wall, listening for any hint that they'd spotted her. But no one was coming this way, all the attention was on the car, on Mike and his baggage. She waited a minute or so, then climbed the side wall into another front yard, crossing it keeping low, and climbing the next wall. And so on, across low garden walls. Stopping every so often to listen, she dared not look back. There was nothing she could do for Mike. Being seen would get her picked up too.

Then over a garden wall and into a side road. She walked

swiftly, upright again, she was out of sight, but still had to take care; a police car could shoot round. Mandy turned down the first street she came to, then again, this way and that, meandering away. Rapidly, she lost any sense of direction, hoping she was creating distance and not going round in circles.

She crossed a green space, utterly disorientated. Might it be Beckton Park? Just trees and grass in the dark, paths weaving without a goal. It was then that she spotted Canary Wharf on the Isle of Dogs. Only a couple of miles away, its flashing light on and off like a lighthouse. That was the way to head, west. And then she would hit a main road that she knew.

In ten minutes, following her flashing star, she came out on Prince Regent Lane. And was unsure which way to go along it. She stood with her arms stretched out, her left arm towards flashing Canary Wharf, her right must be pointing east. So she was facing north. The way she had to go.

She walked swiftly, coming to the Newham Way in a while, and recognised the area from her cycling. She crossed the highway by a high walkway, stopping in the middle to gauge what was happening out there, in the clusters of houses. There were spinning lights, as if there was a fairground on a green. The helicopter was back, knowing where the action was now. Even as she watched, a police car, with full siren, came beneath her vantage point, no doubt heading for the melee.

Mandy was on a familiar route, she'd cycled to cleaning customers around here. She continued north up Prince Regent Lane, past the hospital and the sixth form college, considering what best to do. The police had found the body, she could be certain of that. That was the lights, the sirens, the police cars heading in. Why the helicopter was back. It was a crime scene. They would be questioning Mike, quite what he'd say she wasn't sure, she hoped he wouldn't implicate her, though why should he? It wouldn't help him. And she could deny ever being there. She suddenly realised she was still wearing the rubber gloves that she'd put on to keep her prints off the body. If she were picked up wearing them, that would be a giveaway. Mike would tell enough lies to thoroughly confuse them, once she was home and cleaned up.

They would get his address though. And she'd left her bike there.

She had to be there before they were.

Mandy took off the gloves and put them in a house bin, pushing them far down in the rubbish. She headed for Forest Gate. Walking swiftly, along almost deserted roads, she arrived at the house in about half an hour. There were no police there yet. But there had been a fire next door. The front of the house was black and charred, steaming in the streetlights, the downstairs windows smashed in. Not her problem. Must have happened after they'd left.

So what?

Without further hesitation, she went in the front door, and took out her bike. She hadn't any lights, and so cycled back home on the pavement.

She was only a few hundred yards away, when she heard sirens.

Chapter 37

Once it was ascertained that he wasn't hurt, only dazed, Mike was handcuffed and put in a police car with two uniformed officers. He didn't talk to them, though they'd goaded him about the body in the boot. He was trying to work out what to say, how to get the heat off, if he could, while pretending grogginess.

What a mess!

He watched the goings on from the back seat, as if the outside action were a film, and he was simply a member of the audience in a darkened cinema, as the area was taped off and crime scene investigators began their work. Cops, and who-knows-who, came and went, talking fervently into phones, men and women in white plastic suits as if in a hospital drama were in and around Jean's car. Lights went on in the houses and residents came out in dressing gowns to stand behind the cordon. Police cars were flashing in, sirens blaring, a helicopter hovering overhead.

The two uniformed policemen left him and their places were taken by an Asian male with a notebook, not in uniform, who sat in the driver's seat. Beside Mike, in the back, was a middle-aged, blonde woman without make-up, obviously the senior of the two.

'I'm Detective Inspector Nikki Martin,' said the woman. 'This is my colleague Detective Constable Fayyad Kamani.'

Mike had a headache, his neck was stiff. The handcuffs were cutting into his wrists. They'd found the body. How could they not? Time and fear sobered him. He had to do what he could to get the heat off.

'It's not the way it seems,' he exclaimed. 'No way.' He shifted in the seat, handcuffed, neck aching, it was difficult to get comfortable. 'You've got to believe me.'

'What have we got to believe, Mr Lucas?' said DI Martin.

'I didn't kill her,' he said.

'Kill whom, Mr Lucas?'

'My wife. Jean Lucas.' He took a deep breath, he was shivering, and couldn't have shut up even if he'd thought it was a good idea. These were the people he had to convince. 'It was stupid. I was stoned. I didn't think it was going to go like this.'

'Where were you going?' said Martin.

'I was going to dump her. In the mud, by the Woolwich Ferry. But you have to believe me. I didn't kill her. It's all a mess. It wasn't me.'

'Who did kill her, Mr Lucas?'

'Feliks.'

'Feliks who?'

'Some Polish surname, I can never remember it. He lives next door.'

'So why were *you* carting the body around?'

He took a deep breath. The body damned him, if he let it. Well, he'd put Feliks in the frame, fair and square. But not mention any payment. No way. That would implicate him as the instigator.

'He killed her in my bedroom. In my house, Clova Road, Forest Gate. I found the body about midnight. Big shock. I thought, if I didn't get rid of the body, then you'd think I did it.'

DI Martin suppressed a smile. 'A bit naive, if you don't mind me saying so, Mr Lucas. You should have called us when you found the body. And left us to sort out who did it.' She rubbed her hands together, it was a little cold in the car, the driver's window half down. 'Tell me, how are you so sure it was this Feliks fellow who killed her?'

'He said he was going to.'

'Why would he tell you that?'

'I was having problems with Jean. Rows and money, you

know the stuff, all marriages go through it. I told him about it. He said he'd sort it out for me, permanently. I told him not to interfere.'

'So why do you think he went on to kill her, if you weren't so keen, Mr Lucas?'

'He said he was going to.'

What else could he say? He hadn't killed her, Feliks had. Carting a body around was a crime to be sure, but nothing compared to murder. It was imperative to convince them it was Feliks.

'Feliks said he'd do it. He said to me that I mustn't ask him how or when, and he'd do it. He told me. I said don't do it. He's a spiteful man. We might have been having rows but I didn't want her killed. I said that to him. I didn't think that he would after I told him not to. Just talk. But he went on and did it. He's a madman. I found the body with her head smashed in, up in my bedroom. And thought, I've got to get rid of it. Or the cops will pin it on me.' He had a sudden thought. 'That's what he wants you to think. That it's me, not him.'

'So she was killed in Forest Gate, you say?'

'Yes. I found her in my bedroom. The way he left her.'

'She was certainly not killed here. Not with her head trussed in a black bag. By whom, we've yet to investigate.'

'Not by me. Feliks, I tell you! In my bedroom. Clova Road in Forest Gate.'

'We'll have a chat with Feliks, sir. Don't worry about that. He's high on my list.' She turned to Fayyad who'd been jotting away as they spoke. 'We need to go to the house. If what Mr Lucas is saying is true, it needs to be a crime scene ASAP. Then we'd better pick up this Feliks and see what he has to say for himself.'

'My God!' exclaimed Mike, shaking his handcuffed hands. 'My daughter, Lily. She's only three. She's in the house on her own.'

'Then we'd better go there straight away, Fayyad. And on the way, I'll contact Scene of Crime to get a unit to the Forest Gate address.'

Chapter 38

Jack had slept on the sofa, Mia had the bedroom. It was the way they did things when she was over; the flat only had a single bedroom. He hadn't slept well. Being stood up without explanation had played its various scenarios over and over. He'd had fruitless conversations with Jean; sometimes she'd apologised, sometimes she'd shouted, telling him what a failure he was. For his part, he'd insisted that she could have at least phoned. If she didn't want to go ahead, that was the least she should've done.

The very least.

If Mia hadn't been there, he would have got up in the early hours and gone out. Not a good idea. Where would he have gone? To do what?

He was in the kitchen making breakfast, cooking the remnants from the evening that Jean had stayed over. Two eggs, a couple of slices of bacon, half a can of beans, toast and tea. Busyness was a partial antidote, someone to cook for. The responsibilities of parenthood.

'Breakfast!' he called.

Mia joined him in the kitchen. He scooped the eggs and bacon on to their plates from the frying pan, then spooned out the beans from the saucepan. The toast lay in a heap on a plate in the centre of the table.

'Better than usual,' said Mia. She was in her school uniform, sky blue shirt and navy trousers.

'Make the most of it,' he said. 'I don't think your mum would approve.'

'She wouldn't. Too much fat, nothing green or fruity.'

He half laughed. 'Whenever I see muesli, I think of your mum. It puts me off the stuff.' And then reflected.

'Sorry. I shouldn't say that.'

'It's not news that you quarrel,' she said irritably. 'I've heard you often enough.' She cut her bacon into bits. 'And don't blame muesli.'

'It's too healthy,' he said, knowing it was a stupid thing to say. How can anything be too healthy?

He drank some tea, and put a slice of bacon on a slice of toast.

'What are you going to do about Jean?' said Mia.

He shrugged. 'If she's at the house when I get there, I'll ask her why she didn't show up.'

'And if she isn't?'

'I'll carry on working until she gets there. Then ask her.'

'Will you have a row?'

He was wiping up egg with a slice of toast. 'I'll try not to. Not a lot of point. If she doesn't want to see me, I can't argue her into it.'

'I'm so disappointed in her,' said Mia crunching a piece of toast.

Me too, he thought. He poured out more tea. Though how much was his own fault? Being at too high a pitch. Wanting too much. He should be a Trappist monk, expecting nothing, getting nothing. No surprises or disappointments.

'I wonder how your mother got along with her date,' he said.

'She falls in love far too quickly,' said Mia, taking a sip of tea. 'What do they call it? Sinbad. Single income, no boyfriend and desperate. You must be a Singad. Doesn't ring as well.' She had a thought. 'Sindad! That's much better. Single income, no date and desperate.'

He ignored her chortling.

'Should I try computer dating?' he mused as he wiped toast into his egg.

'Everybody lies, you know.' She was crunching toast,

taking a forkful of bacon between bites.

'I can lie too,' he pondered.

Except he wasn't much good at it. Maybe that was the problem. Feliks had it down to a T. Dress up and tell them what they want to be told. The art of seduction.

'I so wanted to talk to Jean about her book,' said Mia. 'She's a really good writer and I am so broken up that she didn't come.' She took a sip of tea. 'I hope you can sort it out. There has to be a reason.'

'There'll be a reason,' he said. 'Whether I'll want her telling me what it is, is another thing.'

'What do you think it might be?'

He sighed, having been over this too often, but he resisted striking out at Mia. 'That she is going through a heavy divorce,' he said, 'that her husband is being difficult, and this is no time for her to have an affair.'

They ate in silence. All very reasonable, all very true. Except he didn't believe it. Passion didn't care about reasons. The way she had come to him yesterday afternoon, that wasn't a woman thinking ahead, calculating what was best. They'd both seized what was on offer.

Breakfast over, he piled the dirty dishes into the sink. He saw Mia off, her hefty bag on her back. And a few minutes later, he left the house himself.

Chapter 39

Blue and white crime-scene tape traced the front garden wall, going over the gate, deterring unauthorised entry. From the pavement where Jack stood, he could see men and women in plastic protective suits in the hallway.

What on earth was going on?

Next door, much of Feliks's place was blackened, the front door smashed in and the hallway charred. A woman fire-fighter was on the steps in yellow high-vis waistcoat and navy uniform. Saffron's windows were broken, and what he could see of the inside was black and burnt.

Fayyad was by the gate of Mike and Jean's house and beckoned Jack over. His friend was bleary eyed, his suit and shoes covered in plastic protective clothing.

'Hello, Fayyad,' said Jack, bewildered. 'I can't believe all this,' and gestured around him.

'It's all happening on Clova Road, mate,' Fayyad said with a weary smile, looking at his watch. 'A WPC went off to get coffee ten minutes ago...'

'I don't think I'll be working here today,' mused Jack.

'No way, mate.' He chewed his lower lip. 'Maybe tomorrow as you're working on the outside. Most of the crime scene activity is in the house.'

'What on earth has happened?' exclaimed Jack, gazing at the busy people he could see in the hallway.

'Haven't you heard? It's been on the news, radio and TV. The boss was going bananas. Someone tipped off the media.'

'I don't know a thing,' said Jack. 'Just what I see here. Tape and cops. Something big's going on for sure, but I've no idea what.'

'I thought the whole world knew,' said Fayyad. 'That's the bubble I'm in. In short, about two thirty this morning, Mike Lucas, you know him?' Jack nodded. 'Well, he crashed his car after a chase around East Ham and Beckton. And when we caught up with him, we found a body in the boot of his car...'

The air was pressed out of him as if he'd been kicked by a horse in the stomach. It had to be her. She didn't show up, she didn't contact him, they'd found a body. Why wouldn't she have come over last night – unless she was dead.

'The body,' he said holding on to the garden wall, 'Who is it?'

'His wife,' said Fayyad. 'Jean Lucas. Her head smashed in. Mike Lucas, when we questioned him, said it happened here, in the upstairs bedroom. That's why we're here, crawling all over the house. I've been up all night, and I feel like I've been up for a week.' He peered down the road. 'Where is that woman? I need that coffee or I'm going to fall asleep on my feet.'

'When was she killed?' asked Jack, his legs weak, stomach hollow.

'Good question, mate. The pathologist's first estimate is between 3 and 6 yesterday afternoon.'

Couldn't have been 3, Jack knew. He and she were making love in that very bedroom. Or even three thirty as that was when he'd left her. Gone back to work. There'd been the storm and the rainbow. Then he'd seen her go out about four...

He was suddenly aware of Feliks in a smart check blazer and fawn trousers outside next door, staring at the shell of his house, walking up and down bewildered, his fingers running through his thick hair. He strode up the path. The young fire fighter was standing at the top of the steps.

'Sorry, sir,' she said, holding out her hands. 'You can't go in here. It's unsafe.'

'It's my house,' exclaimed Feliks. 'I live up there.' He indicated the top floor. 'Everything. My clothes and furniture are all up there.'

'Sorry, sir. Too dangerous,' said the fire fighter, arms wide to prohibit him going further. 'If you went into the hallway, you'd fall through the floorboards. We've got our investigations to do and then we're going to board up the place.'

'What has happened? I am away for one night...' He was waving his arms wildly. 'And my house is burnt down.'

'All I can say is that it was most likely arson,' said the young woman. 'But I can't tell you any more than that.'

'What is arson?'

'The fire was started deliberately,' she said.

'Those rat faced Russians, I bet you!' he exclaimed, shaking his fist, just as Fayyad and DI Martin came over.

'Are you Feliks?' said DI Martin. She was wearing plastic whites over her suit, the hood down.

'Yes. Why do you want to know?'

'We wish to ask you some questions, sir,' said DI Martin, showing her warrant card.

'My house, look at my house...' He was pointing it out as if she couldn't see it herself.

'Just a few questions, sir. If you'd like to come and sit in the car,' she said as she led Feliks away.

Jack was left leaning on the wall. He wasn't wanted here. And there was no work to be done.

He set off home.

Chapter 40

Feliks was taken to a police car a little way along the road. He and DI Martin sat in the front, and Fayyad in the back taking notes. They gave him their police identities, and took contact details from Feliks who kept gazing out of the window at his blackened house.

'My colleague will take notes,' said DI Martin. Feliks shrugged and she went on, 'You've been out all night, Mr Bukowski?'

'I've just come back, and look what's happened to my house...'

'Where were you last night?' she asked.

'I stayed with a woman. Her name is Alison Bell. Is that a crime?'

'No, it isn't. Do you know why your house was fire bombed?'

Feliks screwed up his eyes. 'What is fire bombed?'

'It means, sir, the fire was started deliberately, so the fire brigade tell us. Do you have any enemies who might do that?'

'No.'

'Does anyone in your house have such enemies?'

'There's the woman, Saffron. She's a prostitute. All sorts of men come, some very nasty.'

'Why do you allow a prostitute to live and trade in your house?'

He shrugged. 'She has to live somewhere.'

'But why your house?'

'Is it illegal?'

'It may be, sir. Depending how much you are taking from her and whether you are offering any other services, such as protection or pimping. In which case you could be charged with living off immoral earnings.'

'I don't know anything about that.'

'How much are you charging her in rent?'

Felix hesitated. 'I am not sure of the actual figure. I have a number of properties...'

'If you won't say, Mr Bukowski, then we can ask her. Your tenant is in hospital at the moment, but we'll get around to her. An exorbitant rent would not assist your case.'

'I wish to speak to a lawyer on the matter.'

'Are you offering her protection, or bringing her clients?'

'I wish to speak to a lawyer on the matter.'

'Certainly, Mr Bukowski. That's your right.' She stopped, considering what direction to take as Feliks was stonewalling.

'Might I ask a question, Ma'am?' said Fayyad.

'Go ahead.'

'One of your tenants has disappeared, sir,' said Fayyad. 'Mrs Sophie Jackson. What can you tell us about that?'

'I don't know where she's gone.' He flapped his hands. 'She's a confused woman. Old. She's wandered off somewhere. Who knows where?' He kept looking at his house as if hoping the fire bombing might be a hallucination.

'Mike Lucas has informed us that you killed his wife,' said DI Martin.

The Pole was silent for a few seconds, face stiffening as he worked out what was going on.

'Rubbish,' he said at last, 'the money was a gambling debt.'

'Are you saying you won the money from him?'

'Yes,' he said reflecting. Had he told them something they didn't know? Too late to retract. Besides Mike might have told them anyway. 'We played cards, very late. He kept betting more and more.'

'How much did you win off him?'

'Three thousand seven hundred pounds. Something like that.'

'That's a lot of money. Are you sure it wasn't payment to kill Mrs Lucas?'

'Kill her? Why should I?' He stopped, realising what they were saying. 'Are you telling me she is dead?'

'She has been murdered, sir. And Mr Lucas has said it was you who killed her.'

He banged a hand on his head. 'Such nonsense. Total rubbish. I was out all night. How could I kill her? I was with Alison Bell. Go on, phone her. She's a respectable head teacher. I'll give you her number.' He scrabbled in his pockets.

'Mrs Lucas died late afternoon, Mr Bukowski.'

'I know nothing about it. In the afternoon, I was working in my garden laying concrete for my shed. You can ask the builder. He was working up the top of that scaffolding tower. He would have seen me. Mr Lucas is a liar. A bad loser.'

'When did you have this gambling session?'

'Monday night and into Tuesday morning. He was drinking and smoking stuff. It's why he plays so bad at cards.'

'Any witnesses?'

'There were only the two of us.'

'How convenient. But considering your involvement in various matters, Mr Bukowski, we will need a full statement from you at Forest Gate Police Station. Right away, if you don't mind.'

'I do mind. I'm a busy man. I have things to do. My house has burned down. I must contact the insurance company. I don't have time to go to the police station.'

'In that case, I am taking you into custody. We will be investigating your connection with a known prostitute, the disappearance of one of your tenants, and your involvement with Michael Lucas who says you murdered his wife. Quite a damning list, Mr Bukowski. And I have omitted the fire bombing of your house. I am sure you do have enemies, no matter what you say to the contrary.'

'You have no evidence for any of this.' His arms flew wildly. 'You accept the word of a lying druggie over that of a respectable businessman. This is a free country, not the Soviet Union!' declared Feliks. 'I'm not going with you.'

'You don't have a choice in the matter, Mr Bukowski. I am arresting you.'

'I shall see my MP. This is a scandal. You are abusing your powers.'

'I'll give you a complaint form at the station, sir.' DI Martin turned to Fayyad. 'Please give Mr Bukowski the official caution.'

Chapter 41

Jack was laid out on the sofa, as empty as a drum. Last night's mystery was solved. *Jean Lucas is unable to reply at the moment. Please phone later.*

It was no consolation knowing why she hadn't replied.

He should go to the police and inform them he was probably the last person to see her alive. Other than the murderer. But that would not resurrect her. She'd been killed at some time between three thirty and six... If Mike had killed her, then when he and Mia came round last night, he had already done it. That made him an impossibly cool customer. Mike had been annoyed that Jean wasn't back to take Lily off his hands. He'd given them coke to drink. It was difficult to believe he'd murdered his wife, and she was lying upstairs in the bedroom all the time.

Yet six hours later he was driving around with her body in his car.

Did it matter? She was dead. A page suddenly torn from his book. If he'd never met her, he'd be no more alone than he was now, mathematically at least. But she'd come into his life, and he had begun to hope for a different future. A future that had been struck with a hammer like a flawed pot.

She had touched him. They'd had the beginnings of an affair. Violins, soft flutes... This morning, walking to Clova Road, he'd been thinking of what to say to her about her non-appearance, eager for the reason, half sure she would have come if she could.

A future jettisoned. No lives to be explored through tumblesome weeks. Months, years, who could say? But there was no one saying anything at all. All conversation halted at the coffin lid.

This was nothing but self pity. All grieving is, he thought. She's dead. You mourn because you can no longer hold her in your arms.

The phone rang. It was Alison.

'Hello,' he said.

'Mia didn't go to Moira's last night,' said Alison.

'She came to my place.'

'I thought you were going out.'

'It fell through,' he said, not wishing to add more. 'Anyway, Mia doesn't like Moira.' Which he knew he shouldn't be saying, but didn't care.

'She doesn't know what she likes.'

A convenient let out, he thought.

'How was your date?' he asked, making a show of interest.

'Wonderful,' she said. 'He's such a gentleman. He knows how to treat a woman.'

With the unsaid rider that Jack wasn't and didn't. But he wouldn't bite.

'His house burnt down,' he said. So maybe he had bit, but in a different place.

'Whose house?'

'Feliks's house.'

'You know him?'

'He lives in the house next door to where I'm working. He told me he was going to the theatre with a teacher. I guessed who it was.'

'It's a small world.'

'And while he was at your place last night, his house burnt down.'

'That's awful. I must call him straight away. How awful.'

She rang off. Presumably to call her perfect gentleman. He rose, he couldn't stay in any longer. He should go for a walk, get some fresh air.

Jack put on a light jacket and went outside. The sky was a dirty grey, the leaves shaking in the plane trees spaced along the road. It looked like rain. So what? He'd get wet. He ambled, hands in pockets, shoulders hunched, considering where he might go.

He should go to the police station and give a statement. Could be problems, as he knew that the last person to see the victim alive was considered a prime suspect. Did he want to go through that? They would question and counter question him. What motive would they come up with for him killing her?

It wouldn't be money. Jealousy, something like that. That she'd tried to end what had barely begun – and he had struck out.

So why was Mike carting her body around?

He would have to talk to the cops sooner or later. Sooner was better, later would increase suspicion. And they'd find his semen inside her. No arguing with DNA. He'd have to tell them that they'd made love, an hour or two, perhaps as close as half an hour, before she died. And that he'd seen her going out in the rain. Going where? To the person who killed her?

That didn't make sense, if she was found in the bedroom. She must've come back, probably when he'd left.

Jack had arrived at Woodgrange High Street, in the tail end of the morning rush hour, the traffic busy, the air thick with fumes. Drivers whooshing it out, breathing it in. Justice of a sort. But he drove one of the machines himself. Added his dirt to the general.

It was a foul world.

He passed William Hill the bookmaker, one of the four betting shops on this short high street. It was busy inside. All men. Was this to replace love? Companionship, excitement, in those frantic minutes of galloping horses, followed by commiserations – and the next bet. With the family eating bread and butter for dinner and hiding from the bailiffs.

Each shop he passed was a way to lose oneself. The

bakery, the chicken shop, another chicken shop, a pawn shop, the latter so you could continue going to the bakery, the chicken shop and the betting office. While the cars sucked in the exhaust of the vehicles in front.

It was all gobbling and compulsion. Did life have any point beyond entertainment and eating? Work so you could. Steal so you could. Fall in love so you could tell each other you were above such impulses.

The only two in the big wide world.

The cop shop wasn't far. He'd go there, give his statement. Feel important for an hour or so, be poked and prodded. Be asked for witnesses to his whereabouts at various times of the day. See the eyebrows raised at sex in the afternoon.

Jack stood wavering on the corner of Woodgrange and Romford Road. The police station was just past McDonald's, just before Green Street. They'd have an incident room by now, with pictures of Jean in the boot of the car, of the car itself, of Mike. Of who else? Him shortly. The last one to see her.

But there was another place drawing him. It had been drawing him for thirty months and he'd resisted. *The Hudson Bay*. Fifty yards down Upton Lane.

No one gave him more than half a glance as he ordered a pint of bitter. Why should they – a man drinking a pint in a pub. The first in two and a half years. You can say no a thousand times, but you only have to say yes once. That's what they said at Alcohol Halt. One of their many mantras.

Which held no comfort on a cold day.

It didn't taste bad. Not the way sin should taste, of blood and bile. And now he'd imbibed the forbidden, he could do it again. Not that he had any choice. The alcohol invoked memories of alcohol. His system knew what to do. Willpower pickled easily.

After two pints he left the Hudson Bay. He'd recognised a

man from Alcohol Halt and didn't want to talk to him. Why did he need to justify himself, anyway? He could do what he wanted, he was a grown up. A free man. You needed a drink sometimes.

Jack headed up the Romford Road, away from the police station, and towards Stratford. He stopped at the *Live and Let Live*. He hadn't been in there for years. It was still a poky dive. The balding, portly man behind the counter looked as if he consumed too much of the sales. Two pints there, and then looser, easier, he continued on his way to Stratford, stopping off for a pee down a side alley.

Into the cavern of the *Goose* where the Co-op store used to be. He went for a lesser volume of liquid, double whiskies. Bells, his namesake. A Scottish friend told him it was lowland rubbish, but that was alright; he was rubbish too, and why get drunk on some single malt that was three times the price, when he was damned if he could tell the difference.

Into the *Goldengrove*. The name from a poem by some poet who'd lived round here once. The words on the wall danced and he had to read them with his finger like a five year old:

Margaret, are you grieving
Over Goldengrove unleaving?

Grieving was for chumps. He would never grieve. Everything dies, he told the man next to him. Who for some reason argued that not everything did, giving as an example the idea of liberty. It will die with you, Jack recalled shouting. The whole world will die with you, he'd insisted. And almost hit the man to prove it.

It was the last thing he remembered.

Chapter 42

Mandy was making him a coffee, Fayyad's fifth of the morning. He was in her sitting room, having been sent over to question her, hoping he was awake enough to make sense of any answers.

The case was confusing. Not helped by lack of sleep. He flicked through his notebook while she was in the kitchen. What had they learned?

Mike Lucas had crashed his car at around two thirty in the morning, and the body of his wife was found in the boot. That was clear enough. Where it started to become cloudy was the time of death. Somewhere between three and six yesterday afternoon. Mike said that at that time, he'd been at his mother's with his daughter. Fayyad had phoned his mother about an hour ago, and she'd agreed that her son had been there. She said he'd left about five thirty. So Mike had an alibi as he could hardly get back from Romford in time. And he had his three year old daughter with him. His mother would have to make a statement but if she stuck to her timing, then Mike was unlikely to be done for murder. Obstructing the course of justice maybe, but not the big M.

Mike said he'd arrived home about six thirty. And he hadn't had cause to go up to the bedroom, where presumably his wife's body lay. And would lie for another six hours. In the meantime, Jack and his daughter came round. Jack needed to be questioned, but Fayyad couldn't get through on the phone. After that, Mike had had a visit from Saffron Baldwin, the pro from next door. They'd smoked weed for an hour or so, and she'd gone home, only to end up rescued by the fire brigade a few hours later. She was now in Newham General kicking up a fuss. In need of a fix, but too ill to leave. Useless to question her in that state.

And then there was Feliks. Fayyad had a feeling about him. Always dangerous, feelings. They can land you in a lot of trouble. But his house had been fire bombed, one of his tenants had disappeared, and Feliks had taken a lot of money off Mike, which Feliks insisted was a gambling debt. What would Mike Lucas have to say about that?

But Feliks himself claimed he was lily white. Fayyad knew, just knew, he was lying about so much. He had to be involved. What about evidence? suggested his boss. Feelings don't go down well with juries.

And other sarcastic remarks. He liked DI Martin. But she had quite a tongue.

Mandy brought in the coffees on a tray, with a plate of biscuits. She placed them on the low table and sat beside him on the sofa. If he'd been wider awake, he might have felt a little uncomfortable being so close. But she'd be mad to make a play for him.

'I always buy Maryland cookies,' she said pleasantly, holding up one of the round, chocolate chipped biscuits. 'It's where I live, Stratford, Maryland. Did you know that Maryland is one of the few places in the UK named after a place in the US? It's nearly always the other way round.'

'I didn't know that,' he said, frankly not knowing much about anything in his current state.

'Someone or other went over to Maryland in America in the 18th Century,' she went on, chattily, 'came back and named his estate here after where he'd been.' She finished triumphantly. 'There you are. A good quiz question.'

'Interesting.' He rubbed his eyes with his fingers. 'Excuse me, but it's been a long night.'

'I'm sure,' she said, drinking her coffee.

'I have some questions for you, Mandy,' he said. 'If you don't mind.'

'No problem.'

'They concern your relationship with Mike Lucas...' He stopped, then added, 'Do you know what's been happening?'

'I did watch the news on TV a little while ago. I saw Mike has been arrested, but I'm confused about what for.'

'He crashed his car in Beckton, or rather his wife's car. And she was found dead in its boot.'

'Oh, that's awful.' Her hand went to her mouth. 'I can't believe it. Did he kill her? I should think he must've done or why carry her body around. I suppose he meant to dump her somewhere.'

'We are investigating the possibilities,' said Fayyad. He yawned. 'Excuse me, but I'd just gone to bed last night, had barely an hour's sleep when I was called out to Beckton.' He sipped some coffee. It was still too hot.

'I heard there was a car chase,' she said.

'There certainly was. Four police cars involved and a helicopter. There was no chance of him getting away, but he was driving like a maniac.'

'Which is why he crashed,' she said.

'That's the background anyway. A body and a suspect. So back to the questions.' His notebook was on his knee. He'd put the coffee back on the table to cool. 'Could you tell me the last time you saw Jean Lucas?'

Mandy half smiled. 'Oh dear, it's all going to come out now. You know I was their cleaner?' Fayyad nodded. 'Well, she caught me and Mike in bed together the day before yesterday. And that was the last time I saw her. Not that I'm not sorry for what's happened to her, but she did get me sacked. A blessing in disguise I suppose. I want to get back to musicals. I'm a singer and dancer, sometimes actor. Unemployed. I must phone my agent and look through the ads.'

'We'll need to take your fingerprints,' he said.

'Of course,' she said with a shrug. 'You'll find them all over the house. I've been cleaning there for a couple of years. I only use gloves for the wet jobs. You'll find them in her car too. She asked me to clean the inside the other day.'

He jotted down the gist. He really should learn shorthand.

'How long has your relationship with Mike Lucas been going on?' he said when his notes had caught up.

'I'd hardly call it a relationship. Friendship perhaps. We worked together in the musical *Liverpool Lullaby*. I only slept with him on Monday, well it wasn't meant to happen, but he had this skunk, really strong stuff. I shouldn't have taken any, not when I'm working. But I did, and whoosh, did it ever hit me! And we ended up in bed. It's not a regular thing. I'm hardly his girlfriend.'

'He said you were.'

'Let's say friend. I wouldn't say lover. Not that often, anyway. One thing you ought to know about Mike, he has too much time on his hands. Doesn't know how to handle it. And it's like she's his boss.' Mandy corrected herself, 'Was his boss, I mean. He didn't like that. Not at all. Hated being kept by Jean. And didn't she remind him every day. According to him, anyway.'

Fayyad couldn't think what else to ask her. There should surely be other things, but he had no idea what. Too many drowsy brain cells. He knew he was doing this badly, that he'd have to come back. Two days in the job and he couldn't question a witness properly. Just as well Mandy was only peripheral to the case.

Chapter 43

When Jack first woke up it was dark. He suspected he'd peed himself, but was wet all over, so wasn't certain. Feeling around told him he was under a bush somewhere, his head hammering, guts fluid. There was a small bottle of spirits lying nearby, about a third full. He sank the rest. And soon afterwards, dropped off.

When he woke again, it was light. Too light. Increasing his headache. He was busting for a pee. He staggered up and pissed behind a tree. Relieved, his consuming thought was alcohol. Jack felt in his pockets. Where was his wallet? He went through every pocket, searched the ground. Either he'd been robbed or he'd left it somewhere.

He came out from the shrubbery and on to the wide path and recognised where he was. In West Ham Park. He must have got in before they'd shut last night. He had no memory of that at all. The last thing he could recall was having an argument at the *Goldengrove*. He couldn't remember what about. Yes, he could, grieving. He'd said some potty things. In vino stupidity.

Sobriety was not an option. He needed his wallet. There was a chance it would be at the *Goldengrove*. And if so, he could pick it up and get a drink. He headed towards the park gate. An old woman with a fox terrier stared at him as he passed. What on earth did he look like? And so what? He was not entering a beauty competition.

He stopped. His motion had disturbed the balance of his stomach. To speed the inevitable, he thrust two fingers down his throat, and out poured a glutinous liquid, patchy white and bubbly. His mouth was sour, he tried licking away the taste. And walked on.

Outside the park, he sat on a low wall, half in the world, but wanting not to be in it at all. Mother booze was his comforter. She had all the answers. He was becoming too sober and didn't like the world he was seeing.

What day was it? He remembered a night, or thought he did. And before that a series of pubs. And before that... Right, that was it. Jean had died. Murdered. Was it Mike or some other clown? It didn't matter. She was dead. He wanted to be dead too.

Better get to the pub then.

At the *Goldengrove*, they looked at him with distaste, as if they'd had no part in him getting in this state. And no, they didn't have his wallet. He wanted to use their toilet which they weren't happy about.

'I'm just getting rid of your watery booze,' he told them. And headed for the toilet.

They would have had to manhandle him to stop him, and they let him go. He emptied his diarrhoea, pee, and vomit. And washed his face. His jacket was muddy, his trousers wet. So what?

He left the pub. No money, so couldn't get drunk unless he begged for change. Aimless, he went into St John's churchyard and laid out on the grass. The sun was shining; he was beginning to dry out, physically at least. He was thinking a little more clearly, but his head was ringing like a bell.

He might have some money at home. Jack searched his pockets. At least he had his keys. He sat up, and recalled that yesterday he'd been going to go to the police station. And remembered why. He was the last person to see Jean alive, other than her murderer. He'd seen her leave the house about four o'clock.

What day of the week was it? He'd asked himself that before. See if he could work it out. Monday he'd gone to work at Jean's place. She'd come over in the evening and they'd gone to look at the conjunction of Venus and Jupiter, he, she and Mia. He smiled when he remembered Mia and Jean arm in arm while he pushed the pushchair. Just like a family. Tuesday, they'd made love. And she was due over at his house, but hadn't come because she was dead. He didn't find out till Wednesday morning when he went in to work and found the house was a crime scene. Then he'd set off for the cop shop and instead gone to the *Hudson Bay*, and a few other pubs, and somehow ended up in West Ham Park. So today must be Thursday. He looked at the church clock. 10.55 and it must be morning, or it would be dark.

Jack rose. He would go home. There might be money there, there was a bed at least. He didn't need food; his stomach wouldn't hold it. Home, the destination gave him purpose. He crossed the main road by the library. There was a memorial for that poet. He looked at the plaque. Gerard Manley Hopkins. What were those words he'd read last night? *Margaret, are you grieving*... He couldn't remember any more. Or say why Margaret was grieving.

He might look it up, but most likely wouldn't.

He crossed Morrison's car park, to go home through the back streets. With his wallet gone, he'd have to cancel his credit cards. How much money did he have in the wallet? He had no idea after his spending in assorted pubs yesterday. Better if he didn't know, then he could assume it was next to nothing.

He'd turned on to Water Lane when he heard someone call.

'Jack!'

There was a woman crossing the road and coming towards him. He vaguely knew her. She was carrying a litre of milk. Of course, it was Mandy. The woman with the bike, the one Jean had thrown out.

'Hello,' he said.

'You look pretty rough,' she was eyeing him quizzically.

196

'It's a complicated story,' he said, knowing it wasn't that complicated really.

'Lots has happened since we last met,' she said. 'Shall we compare notes?'

'It's been a busy couple of days,' he said.

'Come in for a coffee,' she said. 'I only live up the road.'

PART FOUR:
A VIEW FROM THE TOWER

Chapter 44

'A policeman came to see me yesterday,' Mandy said. 'A young Asian guy. Nice chap. Half asleep.'

She had made the coffees which they were drinking seated on her sofa. The room was small, cosy, a little untidy for a cleaner. There was a book open on the table, it looked like a play. A laptop by it, similar to Jean's.

'I know the guy,' he said, not adding any more, too many words.

'He asked me about Mike,' she said, 'but he didn't stay long.'

'Mike's in trouble,' said Jack, sipping the coffee. Too hot. He'd added extra sugar and wondered if his stomach would hold it. He put the cup down, noting a wooden chest across the room. A bit of material was sticking out with a button showing.

'I saw it on the news,' she said. 'And the cop who came confirmed it. Mike's in a mess. He crashed the car with Jean's body in the boot. That's pretty stupid.'

He couldn't disagree. If you have a body in the back of your car, make sure not to crash it. Commonsense.

'He's been arrested,' he said. 'But he may not have killed her.'

'Then why would he be so dumb to be caught carting her corpse around?'

He looked at her. Wasn't she Mike's girlfriend? She wasn't unattractive, a full body, shapely legs. Not a lot of support for Mike now that he was in trouble. But then murder wasn't like a bit of weed dealing.

'Maybe he found her dead,' he said, 'and thought he'd be arrested for it.' Trying to work it out on the fly.

'He should've called the police,' she said.

She'd come closer on the sofa. He wondered whether she was going to make a play. Mike gone, she was unemployed; sex passed the time. Jack might've been up for it but his stomach most surely wasn't. Would it be a denial of Jean? She is dead, rang the big bell of libido.

This morning, though, he could double for a eunuch.

She put a hand on his thigh. This could get difficult, he thought. He could say he had a headache. True, but as an excuse it was used too many times to be believed. Syphilis then, crabs, genital warts.

He said, 'Can I use your toilet?'

She gave him directions and he left the room. It was genuine, even if a momentary let out. He vomited in the loo, next to nothing was expelled but his stomach still retched. He sat on the toilet and emptied his too-liquid bowels. The more he got rid of the better he was likely to feel, surely?

Jean's coat. It came to him. The button on the bit of material sticking out of the chest. She'd worn it when they went out to see the conjunction. She was wearing it when she left in the rainstorm, the last time he'd seen her.

What was it doing here?

He washed, looked in the mirror, and apologised to his body. When he came out she had the book on her lap.

'Work. My audition piece,' she said. 'I have to learn it for tomorrow. Sing a song, dance.'

'Any chance you'll get it?' he said.

She shrugged. 'A chance. The same director me and Mike had for *Liverpool Lullaby*... Do you want to see some photos?'

'Yes,' he said, as one does.

She left the room. Quickly, he went to the wooden chest and opened it. It was the coat. He pulled it out, looked around wildly. Then opened the window a foot or so. He pushed the coat out. And had just time to close it and the chest before she returned holding an album.

They sat at the table and looked at photos of *Liverpool Lullaby*. There were pictures of Mike at keyboards and with a guitar. And Mandy. She was quite a dancer, high stepping and sexy. She told him the photos were from eight years ago, when the show first started, professional stuff. And she'd had copies made for her CV.

'Can you still dance like that?'

She smiled suggestively. 'Would you like to see?'

'I'd love to,' he said. He looked at where his watch would have been. Lost that too. 'But I've an appointment with a customer. Can I come back this evening?'

'Come at eight,' she said.

'Will do,' he said, rising. 'And we'll dance.'

She saw him to the front door. He wished she hadn't as he wanted to get the coat which had dropped down behind the bins. It was raining.

'Have an umbrella,' she said. 'Bring it back tonight.'

And handed it to him. He recognised it at once. It was Jean's. The one she'd had up when she was scurrying off in the rain.

She kissed him on the mouth. They embraced for half a minute.

'Must go,' he said, pulling away.

She waved him away. And went inside. He went down the road a little way and then crept back to rescue the coat from behind the bins.

Chapter 45

'Can I speak to Detective Constable Fayyad Kamani?' he said.

Jack was at Forest Gate Police Station speaking to the desk sergeant. He'd folded the umbrella in the porch of the station, and was holding the coat over his arm.

'On what business, may I ask, sir?' said the sergeant. His shirt was overpoweringly white, his aftershave almost stinging Jack's own cheeks.

Jack half whispered, there were others waiting seated in a semi circle of chairs, 'The murder of Jean Lucas. I've evidence for him.'

The sergeant snapped into professional mode. 'I think he's in the Major Incident Room, sir. I'll just check for you. What's your name?'

'Jack Bell.'

The sergeant phoned through, and told Jack that Fayyad would be down shortly. Jack sat down, and gazed idly at the posters around the walls. For drunken driving. Don't. Using mobile phones while driving. Don't either. Have you seen this man, do not approach him...

Fayyad came out. He was beaming and held out his hand.

'Where the hell have you been, Jack?'

'It's a long story,' he said sheepishly. 'I've got important information about the case.'

Fayyad nodded. 'Come this way, mate. We'll find somewhere private.'

He led Jack through a door and into the sanctum of the station. Along the corridor, he found an empty room. It was small and bare with a table and a couple of chairs, the windows frosted. They sat down.

'Spill, mate.'

Jack began a little incoherently, telling his friend about that last afternoon, two days ago now, when he and Jean had made love. And he had gone back to work, leaving her. About half an hour later, he had seen her rushing out in the rain.

'In this coat and this umbrella,' said Jack, holding up the items.

'Where did you get them?'

'From Mandy. Mike's girlfriend.'

'What was she doing with them?'

'I've been thinking about that on my way here,' said Jack. 'And I think it wasn't Jean leaving the house that I saw, but someone who wanted me to think it was Jean.'

'Why would she want you to do that?'

'Why do you think?'

'Because she was up to no good,' mused Fayyad. 'Which could have been stealing, like the coat and whatever, or, dare I say it, murder.'

'If she knew Mike was at his mother's for the afternoon...'

'Which he could very well have told her.'

'So she came to steal, to get her own back for getting the sack.'

'But Jean came back early...' He stopped and smiled broadly. 'We'd make quite a team, Jack. You should be a detective.' He looked him over, pursing his lips. 'Bit scruffy though. More like a housebreaker.'

'Don't knock it, mate,' he said, pointing out the gear he'd brought with him.

'I'm not, I'm not,' exclaimed Fayyad. 'I am intensely grateful.' He took up Jean's coat and was examining it. 'I went to see Mandy Taylor yesterday. And what a dog's breakfast I made of that interview. The boss gave me such a tongue-wagging, threatening to put me back in uniform... But I tell you, Jack, I was so shagged out...' He stopped.

'What's this?' He was feeling the lining. 'Something's in here.' He put his hand in the coat pocket. 'There's a hole, something's slipped through...' Using both hands, grimacing, he worked on getting it out. 'Probably get a trouncing for this too, getting my DNA all over the evidence... Can't be helped.' And was suddenly triumphant. 'Gotcha!'

He held up a small pen drive.

'I'm going to leave you for five minutes, Jack. I'm just taking this stuff up to the incident room. And we'll see what's on this drive. I'll get someone to make you a cuppa.'

'No, make it a glass of water.'

Fayyad left him.

Jack had vomited once on the way to the police station, but had been OK since. Hopefully, his guts had settled down. There was nothing to come out at either end. His headache had almost gone.

He thought about work. If the police let him, he could finish off the pointing that he'd started yesterday. If the rain had stopped. It was impossible to tell in this room, the window glass frosted. He'd chiselled out the decayed mortar, and had still to fill it. And that was all he was going to do. Jack had had an upfront payment, but knew there wasn't going to be any more. His client was dead. And Mike was going inside for X years for trying to cover up a murder. Which may very well have been done by his girlfriend.

Who'd end up with the house and Jean's money? Lily perhaps. He and she got on well, but she wouldn't be signing any building contracts for a few years yet.

A WPC dropped in with a glass of water and a Danish pastry, the cream spilling out the sides.

'Courtesy of Fayyad,' said the woman with a smile. 'He doesn't do this for everyone. You must be special.'

'We played cricket together at school,' said Jack. 'Quite a bowler, and not bad at the crease...'

'He plays for the Met first team,' said the WPC. 'Bats at number three. Decent spin bowler too. That's why his boss likes him. She's an umpire.' She gave Jack a secret smile. 'Like the Freemasons round here.'

And she left him.

He pushed the pastry aside. The gesture was appreciated, but if he ate it, it would end up in a pool of vomit.

It seemed an age since Fayyad had left. He had no watch, but it must be a lot more than five minutes. Had he been abandoned? Busy place, this cop shop. All these rooms with suspects being knocked about, glamorous pathologists running in with results, the big cheese holding another press conference... Or suchlike.

Fayyad dashed in. 'Sorry about that, mate.' He sat down breathless. 'But I had to fill 'em in on what you'd been saying, to make any sense of the coat and umbrella. Then we looked through the pen-drive. And that was the real identifier.'

'What was on it?'

'Three of Jean Lucas's book covers,' he said with a broad smirk. 'I'm back in the guv'nor's good books. Plus a file for a book Jean was working on. Quite a long thing, over a hundred thousand words.'

'That's the trend these days. Big, fat books.' Or so Mia had informed him.

'More important, mate, was the time that file was last worked on.' He waited, like a comedian timing his punch line.

'Come on. Tell me when.'

'Twelve fifty-four, Tuesday afternoon. I wonder how the young madam is going to explain that. They've sent out a team to pull Mandy in and search her place.'

'Jean was doing her writing in the morning,' said Jack. 'So she must've packed up at 12.54. Then we had lunch together.' He snapped his fingers. 'Just before you got there to question her.'

'Then what? Give me the sequence of her movements.'

'She left about two to visit some childminders. I thought she was going to be out all afternoon...'

'So presumably did Mandy. If she was watching the house, she saw Jean leave...'

Jack nodded. 'My thinking too.'

'The dream team!' Fayyad punched the air.

'Jean came back early, about two forty-five... I saw her, and you know...'

'Mandy still there nicking stuff, thinking she had all afternoon.'

'We'd made love, chatting, in the bedroom, till about three thirty.'

'So where was Mandy while you were shagging the client?'

'That's what I've been thinking. Why didn't she leave?' He shrugged. 'We were totally occupied; we wouldn't have heard a bomb go off in the next room.'

'Must be,' pondered Fayyad, 'that she couldn't leave.' Fayyad snapped his fingers. 'She was in the bedroom. You two rushed in tearing your clothes off... And she just had time to hide.'

'Under the bed? Could she really have been there, all the time?' He reflected. 'We certainly didn't look. Being busy, as it were.'

'Got to be that she couldn't leave,' said Fayyad. 'You two going at it hammer and tongs.'

'I left the bedroom at around three thirty, leaving Jean still in bed, she was having a snooze, going to have a shower... I went back to work.'

'And Mandy came out. And either knocked Jean on the head while she was asleep, or Jean woke up and Mandy clobbered her in panic.'

'Jesus.' Jack wiped his face with his hand. 'And all the time I was up top of the tower pointing. Or under the umbrella sheltering from the rain.'

'Mandy having done her dirty work,' went on Fayyad, 'knows that she mustn't be seen by you. So she takes advantage of the rain, puts on Jean's coat, and goes out under cover of Jean's umbrella.'

'I wondered why she didn't look up and wave,' said Jack dolefully. 'Lord God help me. It wasn't just a quick bang, mate. I was falling for her.'

'Sorry, Jack.' Fayyad patted him on the shoulder. 'I know it's painful going over this.'

'We clicked,' he said. 'My daughter thought she was ace.'

'Don't you want this cake?' said Fayyad, indicating the Danish pastry. 'I bought it for you specially.'

Jack waved a hand. 'You have it. I've been out drinking; my stomach's a wreck. Thanks for the thought, but I'd only throw up.'

Fayyad took the pastry. He took a bite, leaving cream on his upper lip.

'We have the story,' he said. 'We know she's been telling lies. But do we have enough evidence to prove it?'

Jack snapped his fingers. 'I saw a laptop at her place. I bet it's Jean's.'

'How will she explain that?' exclaimed Fayyad. 'They'll have arrested her by now. We'll be all over her flat, mate. See what else she's got. Don't you worry. Now, if you don't mind, I've got to take a full statement from you. Forget all our supposition, about what Mandy was doing or not doing. Leave that to us now. I just want to know about your actions.'

Chapter 46

Jack gave his statement. It took them a couple of hours to go through it all. And during that time, his headache eased away. He needed one toilet break but was no longer vomiting. Near the end, he was able to take tea and biscuits, and would have welcomed the Danish pastry if it had still been on offer.

Fayyad had to write the statement in longhand. Jack was surprised at the laborious system.

'It's so no one can mess around with it afterwards,' Fayyad explained.

The statement began from the time when Jack had come to work at the house, covering Mike and Mandy lumbering him with Lily while they went upstairs, his first meeting with Jean when she'd harangued him for looking after Lily, and his witnessing Mandy's ejection, through to the evening on Wanstead Flats with Mia, Lily and Jean. And finally, the next day at lunch with Jean, their love making when she returned early, his going back to work, and apparently seeing her leaving the house in the rain.

Fayyad left Jack to read through the lengthy statement and to sign each page to say it was correct. After quarter of an hour, Fayyad returned with sandwiches for them both and mugs of tea.

'A good morning's work,' said Fayyad, taking the plastic off his sandwich. 'They're interviewing Mandy in one room, Mike in another. He's now claiming she was with him in the car last night. Wouldn't surprise me. We did wonder how he got the body in the car by himself, half stoned. Scene of crime people are working like beavers. One team over at the car wreck, another at the Clova Road house, and a third at Mandy's place on Water Lane. You were right about that laptop. It's Jean's. There's some jewellery, too, that we suspect isn't Mandy's.'

'What's happening to Lily?' asked Jack.

'She's gone to Jean's mother.'

'I hope she'll be OK. Poor kid. Not talking yet. A sweet thing though. Mum dead, father charged with what?'

'Perverting the course of justice. So far.'

After their lunch, Fayyad checked that Scene of Crime had finished where Jack was working. They had, but were still in the house. He offered Jack a lift over which he accepted. Might as well work as feel sorry for himself at home. Or worse.

The rain had stopped, the sun was out amidst fast moving white clouds. He always felt more positive in the sunshine. He should contact Max about his fall from grace. And must report his lost credit cards. Soon as. Soon as.

'They're digging up Feliks' shed foundation,' said Fayyad as he drove.

Jack laughed. 'That'll annoy him no end. Personally, I doubt you'll find anything.'

'Why's that?'

'Too obvious.'

'Could be a double bluff,' suggested Fayyad.

Jack reluctantly agreed.

They had to park some way from the house, and walked up. Feliks' house now had plywood boards bolted over the ground-floor door and windows. Secure enough, thought Jack. It all makes work for the builder.

'What's happened to Saffron?' he asked.

'She ran off from the hospital early this morning. We don't know where she is now. Which could kibosh our case against Feliks. We were hoping to get him for living off immoral earnings.'

'Why are you so keen to dig up his concrete? You think Mrs Jackson might be there?'

'Spot on. She's a homebody, according to her son, but nowhere to be found. So we suspect foul play.' He smiled. 'I've got to go and see how they are getting on with the dig.'

'I can hear the drilling,' said Jack. 'Put on ear muffs, mate. He's laid down a lot of concrete.'

'You really must come up to Ilford and meet the family, Jack.'

'Give me a date. I'm totally free.'

They arranged it for Sunday afternoon. Jack and Mia were invited for lunch. If the weather was fine later, they'd get a boat out on Valentine's Park lake.

They parted. The detective went down Feliks' garden to see what was happening with the drilling. Jack went to the shed down the end of the other garden. There, he put on his overalls and helmet. He trowelled cement into a bucket, and took this and another bucket to the outside water tap at the edge of the patio.

There he saw the mix in a bucket, that he'd made up two days ago. All the rain had caused the mortar to set in the bucket, as water had leaked in at the edge of the plastic sheet he'd laid on top. Just as well he had extra buckets. That one was only good for throwing out.

He'd need to check the tower. Jack climbed up, and section by section, made sure the joints were tight. With his fragile head, the noise of the drilling was a pain, even this far off. It must really annoy the neighbours, he thought. First they'd had the cement mixer chugging endlessly on, and now the drill hammering away to take up what Feliks had been putting down.

At least his headache had almost gone.

Going down to ground level, he carried the fresh bucket of cement out front, where he trowelled in sand, and dolloped in a rough measure of plasticizer. Jack mixed the components and took the buckets to the tap on the patio, adding water slowly to the mortar mix. Too wet and it would seep out of the course, too dry and it would be too crumbly to work with. He half filled the other bucket with water to keep his brickwork wet, and took them to his tower. One at a time, he hoisted them to the top.

This was his own time, his own money. The last work he'd be doing at the house. There was no one to pay him to do any more. He'd had half the payment and that was all there was going to be. Then he had a thought. He could claim off Jean's estate. It would take ages to sort out, with Jean murdered, and her husband in jail. Might take a year to sort out. But he'd be a creditor. He had the contract she'd signed. The work still needed doing.

Worth considering. Work was his salvation, giving structure and purpose to his day. And while working he couldn't be drinking. Even if he didn't get paid for a year.

But while he had nothing else on, why not carry on with the job?

Yesterday was meltdown. For two and a half years, he hadn't touched the stuff. And then he was shafted when he'd learnt about Jean. One drink, that was all it took to get him on the road to oblivion. He'd lost all sense and his wallet too. The latter maybe just as well, as he had no easy means of getting cash. There was food at home, plain stuff, to keep him going till the weekend when Mia was coming over.

In the meantime, stay dry. Go to Alcohol Halt this evening.

He pressed mortar in the courses. He'd got the knack, taking just the right amount off the mortar board with the trowel and scoring it along. Then, once the trowel was empty, going back along the line to get the finish. Easy, once in the rhythm.

His phone was a worry. He hoped he hadn't lost that too. It was possible he'd left it at home before he went out drinking. The number was on his business cards and website. All that hassle and expense if he had to replace it.

Had someone found him comatose and robbed him? Or had he dropped his wallet somewhere? Cross fingers and hope his phone was on the table at home.

The drilling had stopped. There was a skylark somewhere, that rapid, high trill. There it was, he could see it just above the rooftop, hovering and rising, its wings flapping like mad. He should've brought his binoculars up here with him. Maybe not. The neighbours would report him as a Peeping Tom.

He'd cheered up. Sunshine, the skylark, the easy movement with his hand and trowel. How important work was. Especially at this time with Jean dead. She'd been killed in the bedroom, so soon after they'd made love. They'd chatted for ten, fifteen minutes, who was counting, talking about things they might do together. A walking holiday in Cornwall was suggested.

And all the time Mandy was there. Under the bed. There wasn't anywhere else to hide in the room. If only he'd spotted her. In some other universe, somewhere, he had done so, and she'd run for it. And still naked, he'd caught her halfway down the stairs.

There'd be a funeral, in a few weeks, most likely. Arranged by Jean's mother. Lily would be there all dressed up, not understanding what was going on. Mike would be in custody awaiting trial. Mandy too. And he would be on another job hopefully, not even knowing the funeral was happening. Unless he decided to finish off here.

It'd not be the happiest of jobs, if he did decide to continue. Every day reminded of Jean, going in to the house, to go to the loo, to make a coffee.

The funeral didn't matter much, whether he'd be invited or not. Now was the pain. He'd opened up to her, and must shut down again. The dreams were smashed. Accept, pal. He'd make a good agony aunt. So easy to tell other people what to do.

The drill started up again. Irritating. The sound broke through his thoughts. He turned and watched from his high vantage point. The man with the drill was juddering as his machine thumped the concrete. He wore a hi-vis yellow waistcoat, earmuffs, goggles and gloves. Sensible fellow. He'd seen plenty too careless of their health and safety.

He half laughed. Who was he to lecture anyone after pouring in the poison yesterday?

The driller was a workman, taken on ad hoc by the police. There was another in a similar waistcoat, helmet and goggles, leaning on a pickaxe, waiting his turn. Three plain clothes police officers were standing some way back. There was Fayyad, his boss, and a third woman who Jack presumed was a cop too.

Out of mortar, he took a breather. And looked about, leaning on the railing. He was up with the rooftops. There were still a few runner beans on the plants on Feliks' poles down there, some tomatoes. Other greenery he couldn't recognise from this height, and maybe wouldn't know at ground level either. And a patch, ovalish, darker than the surrounding soil. All that rain must have heightened it.

He took advantage of a break in the drilling, and yelled, 'Fayyad!'

His friend looked round, and up at the waving figure at the top of the tower.

'Come up here!' Jack yelled.

Fayyad came towards him, obviously puzzled. The two other officers were looking his way too.

At the bottom of the tower, Fayyad called up, 'What's the problem, Jack?'

'Come up here. I can see something.'

Fayyad climbed the tower, in his suit and shiny shoes. At the top, he brushed himself down.

'What's all this about, getting me to climb up here?'

'See there.'

Jack pointed out to him the dark area in the vegetable garden. The two other police officers had come to the bottom of the tower.

'I do, I do,' said Fayyad excitedly. He called down to his colleagues on the ground, 'Would you come up here, ma'am? There's something of interest for you to see.'

The two police officers climbed up and joined Fayyad and Jack at the top of the tower. Jack stood back as it was quite crowded in the limited space as Fayyad pointed out the oval-shaped patch of darker earth. A few minutes later, the workmen had left their drilling, and were digging amongst the vegetables. They dug for some time while Jack continued with the pointing. He knew if there was anything to be found, Feliks would make sure it was deep down.

Some time later, Jack was on ground level, making up mortar, when he heard a cry from the other garden. He went over to join the police officers around the hole the workmen were digging. They'd uncovered a roll of old carpet, from which a bony hand protruded.

Chapter 47

At home, he found his phone on the sitting room table. One expense spared. There were various messages on it including those from Alison and Fayyad. Fayyad he'd seen since. Alison he'd deal with later. First job was the bank. He phoned them and was able to cancel his two lost credit cards. He was vague about how he'd lost his wallet, suggesting pickpockets, not wanting to admit to being drunk and incapable. He arranged to pick up some cash at the bank the next day, to tide him over until new cards came.

He must get back in the habit of going to Alcohol Halt. He'd taken to skipping sessions as if he were clean and free. But it was never easy getting off the damned stuff. It was everywhere. Every supermarket and backstreet shop, no event could be complete without society's favoured drug. He must learn to deal with unhappiness without booze. Like now, being home by himself, his love dead. He was gasping like a fish on the riverbank.

Jack went into his kitchen. The dirty dishes in the sink greeted him. He ignored them and opened the fridge. And found bread, cheese, some margarine, and the remnants of salad stuff from when Jean had been here a century ago. He wouldn't starve.

His doorbell rang. He went down, and there were Alison and Mia with a couple of pizzas.

'Where on earth have you been, Jack?' exclaimed Alison.

'Out and about,' he said warily.

'Drunk?' she enquired.

'Well...' he began, and stopped. He could either lie or admit it.

'I won't enquire further,' said Alison diplomatically. 'We

brought these takeaways. If you weren't in, we were going to have them at home.'

They came up. Alison went in the kitchen, saying nothing about the mess, simply washing three plates and some cutlery, and taking them into the sitting room.

'We saw it all on TV,' exclaimed Mia. 'How Jean Lucas was found in a car. So awful. No wonder you got drunk.'

Alison gave her a severe look.

'I shouldn't have done,' he said. 'But I did. Drink shouldn't be a fallback for any difficulty.'

'You've done well up to now,' said Mia. 'And when your girlfriend gets murdered... Well, it would drive anyone to drink.'

Alison had opened up the pizzas.

'Help yourself,' she said.

'We thought you might need a boost,' said Mia.

'I'm grateful for the grub,' he said. 'And for the company.'

'Jean was such a nice woman,' said Mia. 'Much better than your other girlfriends.'

'Stop it,' said Alison.

'I was only saying how nice she was. A good writer too.'

They ate in silence for a while. He was pleased to have them here, especially with his drab larder, but he suspected Alison had an ulterior motive.

'Do you know what's happened to Feliks?' she said.

That was it. Sympathy for him, to be sure, but she wanted information.

'I do,' he said, taking a large bite of pizza, to give him thinking time.

'Can you say what?'

He put down his knife and fork, and took a sip of water. There was no easy way to put it.

'He's been charged with murder.'

'Murder?' she cried. 'That can't be true. He's such a gentleman.'

'All a front,' said Jack. 'They found a body in his garden this afternoon. I was there when they dug it up. It's almost certainly Mrs Jackson, his downstairs tenant. Her son is coming tomorrow to identify the body.'

'Are they sure Feliks did it?' said Alison weakly.

Jack shrugged. 'In his vegetable patch. Who else could it have been? The only other person living there, before the fire, was Saffron, who was stoned most of the time.' He stopped, aware he was hurting her. 'I'm sorry to be the bearer of bad news, Alison. But I was on the spot. I saw them find the body.'

Alison sniffed, trying not to cry. 'I've been such a fool. I believed what he told me.' She wiped her eyes with the back of her hand. 'That'll teach me.'

Jack said nothing. He could've said that he'd have warned her if she would ever listen to him. But there was no point, especially when she was so upset.

He said, 'I'm sorry. It's as well you weren't too involved.'

'The police came to the school yesterday,' she said with a sniff. 'They asked me about Feliks. I told them he stayed the night, but the more they asked the more I realised that I knew next to nothing about him.'

'He wanted Mrs Jackson out,' said Jack, 'She was on a fair rent. And Feliks hated that. He's a bastard when it comes to money.'

Aware that he'd used impolite language, he turned to Alison to assuage her reaction, but she didn't react. Murder was a worse word.

Mia said, 'You have to be so careful with computer dating. Everybody says so on Facebook.'

Alison gave a grim laugh. 'I tell my kids all this stuff. Beware of people online. And so on and so forth. And then I get suckered myself.'

'I'll make us some tea,' said Jack.

While in the kitchen, he washed the dishes. It was visitors

219

that made him conscious of such things. Though Alison in her diplomatic mode had said nothing critical. It wouldn't last.

The company was good though. When they'd gone, he'd phone Max. He needed his wise words, though to be exact, he knew every one of them. He wanted someone else to be saying them. On Sunday, he was going to see Fayyad and his family. That was something to look forward to. Mia would be over tomorrow night for the weekend, so he only had to get through the day.

Pull down all the strategies he knew to stay off booze.

He'd go back and finish the work at Clova Road after the weekend. He was contracted to do it. He'd hired the tower, bought the materials. They would have to pay him in the end. He'd have no company though. Except the cops at the crime scene.

They'd leave in a day or two. And there'd be no one. Feliks' place was burnt out, no one there either. Though he had the key to Jean's place. She had a well stocked fridge with no one to eat it. He could help out there. He should bring a radio and earphones.

So finish off at Jean's. Get paid when he would. Out of his control when.

But he needed work that paid now. Not in a year's time. There was enough in his account to tide him over for a few weeks. There was enough food at Jean's to keep him going awhile. So savings there, and decent grub too. Jack knew she wouldn't begrudge it. It would only go to waste. He could phone Bob, do some subcontracting for him. He'd be worth a buzz. And in the meantime, just keep on, up the tower at Clova Road.

Thank you!

I am grateful to every reader who finishes one of my novels. I have taken you on a journey which I hope you have enjoyed. There are plenty of things you could have been doing, other than reading this book. So, thank you for your time.

If you liked **Jack On The Tower**, here's what you can do next:

I'd appreciate a review on Amazon. In that way, you can help me tell other readers about my books. Without reviews authors get few sales on Amazon. So I'd be grateful for your review to help this series get on the move.

You can get a **FREE** ebook of **Jack of Spades** if you sign up for my readers' list. You may give it to a friend if you wish. Every month a lucky reader from the list will be sent a **free**, signed paperback of their choice from the series. Sign up using this link:

http://eepurl.com/buAh5H

When you sign up for my readers' list you will receive my regular newsletter. This will give you news about me, what I'm reading, tell you about my future books, PLUS a variety of giveaways.

Books by DH Smith

DH Smith is the name I use for my Jack of All Trades series. The books are all standalone novels and can be read in any order.

Out Now:
- Jack of All Trades
- Jack of Spades
- Jack o'Lantern
- Jack By The Hedge
- Jack In The Box
- Jack on the Tower

Coming Soon:
- Jack Recalled
- Jack at Death's Door
- Jack at the Gate

Books by Derek Smith

All my books, other than the Jack of All Trades series, are written under the name Derek Smith.

Mystery/Crime
Murder at Any Price

Fantasy
Hell's Chimney
The Prince's Shadow
Elektra

Other
Strikers of Hanbury Street (short stories)
Catching Up (poetry)

Young Adult Novels
Hard Cash
Half a Bike
Fast Food
Frances Fairweather Demon Striker!

Children's Novels
The Good Wolf
Feather Brains
Baker's Boy

For Younger Children
The Magical World of Lucy-Anne
Lucy-Anne's Changing Ways
Jack's Bus

About the Author

I live in Forest Gate in the East End of London. In my working life, I have been a plastics chemist, a gardener and a stage manager before becoming a professional writer. I began with plays, working with several theatre companies, and had a few plays on radio and TV, as well as on the stage. In the early 80s I became involved in running a co-operative bookshop and vegetarian café in Stratford, learning to cook, and having my first go at writing a novel. The first was a mess, and, after too many rewrites, binned. The transition from drama to novels took me a couple of years to get to grips with. My first success was a young adult novel, Hard Cash, published by Faber. Buoyed up by this, I stuck with children's work, did school visits, and made a hand to mouth living as a full time author, topped up with some evening class work in creative writing at City University and the Mary Ward Centre in Holborn. A few adult fiction titles appeared from time to time, between the children's list, and I have since been working more in that direction with my Jack of All Trades series.

My full name is Derek Howard Smith. I write as DH Smith for my Jack of All Trades series; all other books appear under Derek Smith. Earlham Books is my own imprint.

www.dereksmithwriter.com